THE WAITING BRIDE: A REGENCY ROMANCE

THE RETURNED LORDS OF GROSVENOR SQUARE (BOOK 1)

ROSE PEARSON

LANDON HILL MEDIA

THE WAITING BRIDE

CHAPTER ONE

"*I*t be cold today, my lord."

Philip Belmont, Viscount Galsworthy, shivered slightly as though the Captain's words had only just brought to mind how truly cold the air was.

"Indeed," he murmured, glancing at the Captain and taking in the way that the man was staring out at the ocean with a knowing look in his eyes. He did not know much about the ocean but was glad to be sailing with a knowledgeable Captain. "The air has a breath of frost in it."

The Captain chuckled. "It will be autumn by the time we dock on England's fair shores, my lord."

"I find that I am already looking forward to it," Philip replied with feeling. "The heat of India was never something I truly enjoyed, to be frank."

The Captain looked surprised. "I have never heard a man say before, in all of my life, that he prefers a cold wind to a warm breeze, my lord. Unless there is something else that will be warming your bones once you return?" He threw a knowing look in Philip's direction, but Philip shook his head sharply.

"No, indeed not," he muttered, refusing to let his thoughts turn in that direction for fear of what would occur within him if he did so. "The freshness of the air and the coolness of the breeze brings me a good deal of joy, for it reminds me of home."

After a moment, the Captain nodded slowly, his gaze returning to the expanse of the sea. "You have been away from home for some time?"

"Nearly two years," Philip replied, recalling how glad he had been to leave England's shores at the time. "I have been inspecting the holdings in India, but I have no other recourse than to return at this time."

"You are a little reluctant, I think," the Captain murmured, not so much as glancing at him.

Philip exhaled slowly. "Indeed," he muttered, not wanting to give very much away. "But return I shall, regardless of consequence."

At this, the Captain left him to stand on deck alone, battling with his thoughts. It had been more than a year since he had last seen Miss Weston, since he had last pressed her hand and promised that he would return so that they might plan their wedding. He had not felt any desire other than to leave her side, quite sure that their betrothal was not something either of them particularly wanted – even though they had been engaged for some years. Of course, it had been simply a matter of family obligation. His father and hers had wanted to join their family lines together and, as such, he had not been allowed any input on the matter. Neither had she, for that matter, not that she had ever complained to him about it, of course. Not a single word of complaint had ever left her lips, although there had always been an uncertainty in her eyes whenever she had looked at him. The way she so often toyed with a tress of her fair curls had only added to the picture of hesitation that she portrayed. He could see it now, reflected in his mind, that doubt which continued to bite at him, continued to trouble his mind, no matter how often he tried to battle it.

Why had he never spoken to her of it? Was he so afraid of his own late father's dictates, of his own responsibilities, that he had never had the courage to ask her how she truly felt? Perhaps then he might not have felt compelled to run away to India in an attempt to remove himself from the situation.

Of course, the idea had been foolishness itself. To remove to India meant that their wedding plans were only postponed, not forgotten altogether. Besides which, having now come into the title of Viscount Galsworthy meant that he had specific responsibilities at home, which he had entirely neglected whilst in India. Perhaps the idea of leaving England for a time had been to give him time to reflect, time to make himself quite certain of all that he wanted, all he desired. Instead, he was returning to England with as much uncertainty as he had left with, almost dreading seeing his bride-to-be for fear of what he would see in her face.

"Maybe she has found another and will have eloped

by the time I return," he muttered to himself, his mind crowding with dark thoughts. It was not as though Miss Marianne Weston, daughter of Viscount Bridgestone, was not every inch a lady. She was refined, elegant and polite in every way. On top of which, with her bright blue eyes, flawless complexion, and fair hair, she was a remarkably pretty thing, who he would be proud to have on his arm, had he any feeling for her whatsoever.

Groaning, Philip dropped his head. Therein lay the problem. He was quite lost as to what to do, for he did not feel anything at all for the lady. It was not as though he had ever entertained dreams of love, fondness, and overwhelming affection for his wife, having been quite certain that his marriage would never hold such a thing, but he had hoped to feel some kind of connection with the lady. Indeed, whilst he found Miss Weston to be charming and beautiful, the fear of being pressed into a marriage he neither wanted, nor had hoped for, had chased him from her side. There was nothing but fear and doubt between the two of them. Even in the letters which she had written to him, he found nothing and felt nothing. There was no spark to bring a flood of excitement to his heart, no delight to cast him into thoughts of what would be waiting for him when he should return.

Sighing aloud, Philip leaned heavily on the deck, looking down at the waves and feeling the icy wind on his cheeks. Surely there had to be some kind of excitement, simply at the thought of becoming wed to Miss Weston? He closed his eyes and tried his best to feel something good, something wonderful, even just the smallest flicker of delight... but all he felt was dread.

Eventually, having given into the doldrums, Philip made his way down to his cabin, seeing his coat lying across his trunk. Setting it aside, he lifted the trunk lid and saw the stack of letters Miss Weston had written to him over the course of his time in India. He had read every one, of course, and had responded with news of what he was involved in and the like, but had never once mentioned any sort of longing for her company or how much he missed hearing her voice. Nor had she, for that matter, although each letter had ended with the same words: 'Earnestly awaiting your return'.

He unfolded the last one and read it again, wanting desperately to roll his eyes but choosing not to. He did not believe that she was truly missing him, nor that she was, in truth, waiting for his return with eager expectation. But he knew full well that those words were almost expected from a betrothed lady of society. Her father, the rather brusque Lord Bridgestone, would most likely read the correspondence before it was sent, simply to ensure that all was just as it ought to be. He would expect his daughter to make quite clear that she was looking forward to her betrothed's return.

"What am I to do?" he muttered aloud, raking one hand through his hair as he stared down unseeingly at the letter in his hand. The desire for adventure, the desire to escape, had long since passed, but yet his lack of feeling remained the same. What of her? What if her heart had changed in the time that they had been apart?

"That would be a torture indeed," he said loudly, feeling his heart twist in frustration. Placing the letter back with the others, he carefully retied the ribbon around them all, still a little unsure as to why he had not only saved the letters, but had chosen to return to England with them. There was no need for him to do so, not if he was to be in Miss Weston's presence again. His finger traced the ribbon gently, a frown creasing his brow.

A flurry of nerves ran through him as he considered the moment when he would see Miss Weston again. What would he say to her? What was he expected to do? As yet, there had only been the very briefest of touches between them. Surely, she would only expect him to take her hand and bow over it, although he might have to brush a kiss against her knuckles should she appear disappointed at the former. There was no desire on his part to crush her into his arms at the earliest opportunity, desperate to find a quiet moment with her so that he might press upon her just how much he had missed her. One thing Philip was determined not to be was untruthful, neither in word nor action. He would not profess love for her when he felt none in his heart, although he was quite determined to be as loyal and as devoted as a husband ought to be, should the time come. There would be no mistresses for him. He quite reviled the idea, even if his bride-to-be was not a lady he held in his heart.

There came a short rap on his door and, quickly closing the trunk, Philip rose to his feet. Opening the door, he saw one of the cabin boys standing there, looking a little awkward as he held out a tray of food to Philip.

"Thank you," Philip murmured, thinking to himself that the one thing he would be looking forward to, at least, was having a decent meal back in England.

"Oh, and the Captain says to tell you we're in sight of

England," the boy said, looking up at him with uncon-
cealed curiosity. "He thought you might want to know."

Philip felt his stomach twist. "Thank you," he said
again, feeling the color drain from his face. "How long
will it be until we dock?" Setting the tray down carefully,
he turned back to the boy who was still looking up at him
inquisitively.

The boy shrugged his skinny shoulder. "I'd say a
couple of days, my lord." He wiped his nose with a
ragged sleeve and then grinned up at Philip, evidently
hoping to get more than just a 'thank you' from him. "I
can find out from the Captain for you if you'd like?"

Philip nodded his head jerkily and pulled out a coin
from his pocket, which he tossed to the cabin boy. He
caught it deftly and pocketed it at once, his grin
spreading all the more. "I'll go and find out for you right
this minute, my lord."

"There is no particular rush," Philip replied quickly.
"I'll need time to eat." Glancing back at his tray, he found
the food less than appetizing, although he might be able
to stomach the coffee at least. "You can find me back up
on deck later."

"Of course, my lord," the boy said, making a terrible
attempt at a bow that made Philip wince. "Thank you."

Watching the boy run off, Philip closed the door and
felt the ship lurch a little, making him press one hand to
his stomach. He had not become particularly used to the
rolling of the ship even though he had been on it for some
time, but apparently, the Captain said that standing on
solid ground again would feel all the more strange once
they arrived.

Philip would have to simply wait for that moment, his stomach rolling over at the thought of setting foot on England's shores once more. There would be no running this time. In a few short weeks, he would find himself a married man, and from that, he could never escape.

CHAPTER TWO

"*D*o keep up, Hetty!"

Miss Marianne Weston twisted her head to see her maid bustling to catch up with her. She was aware that she was walking rather quickly, but felt no concern over it, telling herself that her maid, who had been with her for some years, ought to be doing all she could to stay in step with her.

"Is something the matter, my lady?"

Marianne rolled her eyes to herself. There was a good deal going on in her heart but that was not something she could easily share with her maid. "Hetty, you need not worry about me. I am quite all right."

"Are you quite sure, my lady?" Hetty asked, still sounding rather anxious. "You have been walking ever so fast and that is usually a sign that you have something pressing on your mind." There was a moment of silence. "Is it that your betrothed is to return to England very soon?" Marianne closed her eyes momentarily. "I can understand that it will be a very exciting time for you once Lord Galsworthy returns," Hetty continued, her voice drifting across Marianne's shoulder as they walked. "The preparations that will need to be made! Oh, I never felt such excitement!"

That remark stung, even though Marianne knew it had not been intended to. She did not feel any of the excitement her own maid felt, struggling to feel anything at all for her betrothed other than worry.

"I must say, I was glad to hear that Lord Galsworthy has a house near to your father's," Hetty sighed, happily. "It will be good for you to stay near to the master whenever you are in London. Although I hear that Lord Galsworthy has a wonderful estate near the coast. Imagine! The sea! I haven't ever seen the sea before."

"Hetty," Marianne said, with a good deal more sharpness than she had intended. "I do not think that you need to consider such things, as kind as it is of you to consider my future."

"Oh, but it is all I have ever hoped for you, my lady," Hetty continued, reminding Marianne just how long Hetty had been with her. "I have always wanted to see you happy and settled, and this Viscount Galsworthy seems to be just the ticket! Handsome, wealthy, and more than able to look after you... I'd say that's one of the best matches you could have made, my lady."

Marianne's lips tightened for a moment in a long, thin line. It was not as though she had been given any choice in the matter. In fact, she could still recall the day her father had called her into his study simply to tell her that she was to now consider herself engaged.

That had been something of a shock. She had only been introduced to Lord Galsworthy on one occasion the previous week, which she had then realized had been deliberate on the part of her father. As she'd stood there in her father's study, a cold hand of fear had clasped around her heart. She knew nothing of Lord Galsworthy and certainly had no expectation of what he would be like as her husband. Was he cruel? Did he have a kind heart? How was she to know? Whilst she had always considered her father a good parent, he had never shown particular interest in her wellbeing, such as it was. Therefore, he had not understood the fears which had immediately assailed her, for he had expected her to behave with gracious thanks and quiet excitement. When she had stated that she did not know the man, that she could not tell what kind of husband he would be, her father had simply waved a hand and assured her that she would rub along quite nicely with her husband, he was quite sure, and that had been the end of the matter. She was to wait for Lord Galsworthy to propose to her, she was to accept and then the news would be made public. Both families were aware of what was expected but the onus still lay with Lord Galsworthy.

How long Lord Galsworthy had known of their betrothal was still something of a mystery to her, for he had not expressed any particular interest in her at their first meeting. It had only been a week after their first introduction that he had sent her a note asking to call upon her. How surprised she had been to discover that he soon intended to go to India, to survey his holdings for himself! It had made sense, she had considered, for he had only just completed his year of mourning for his late father, and had not yet gone to see his holdings in person, but for him to remove so soon after their betrothal had become known to her had been a little astonishing. He had assured her that he would return soon and she had promised to write to him faithfully. They had only had one month of courting – a month filled with reluctant conversation and an air of uncertainty which had wrapped itself around both their shoulders – before he had taken passage to India. Of course, she had done as she had promised and written faithfully every fortnight, ending with the words 'Earnestly awaiting your return' – but she had never received the same in reply. He had sent her some letters, of course, but they had never once suggested that he too was looking forward to being in her presence again.

It was quite clear, in Marianne's mind, that this marriage was not something of Lord Galsworthy's choosing but, like most men of his title and standing did, he had simply accepted it as the future he had no choice over.

She disliked that intensely. Oh, how she wished that she could have enjoyed a season in London, where she might have become acquainted with a good many gentlemen, dancing, and conversing at all sorts of occasions, before being courted by one or two. She might have had her heart stolen away by one of them and would she not have gone into that marriage with a good deal more willingness than this? But now, as things stood, she had very little choice in the matter. Regardless of what Hetty thought, she was not looking forward to her marriage to the Viscount and she very much doubted he was in any way excited by the prospect either.

"Has he proposed to you as yet, my lady?"

Again, Hetty's words tore at her heart. "No, Hetty, he has not," she said bluntly, wishing to goodness her maid would stop asking questions. "I think I should like to walk in silence for a time, to contemplate matters. That is more than enough questions for the moment."

She glanced over her shoulder to see Hetty looking away, clearly a little embarrassed at having been reprimanded so. "Of course, my lady," came the now quiet reply, leaving Marianne to walk in silence.

Unfortunately for Marianne, Grosvenor Square was not particularly quiet, and her mind was now entirely caught up with the knowledge that her betrothed had not yet proposed to her, as had been expected. Before he had removed to India, they had been given a month to allow their courtship to develop but he had not taken the opportunity to propose to her. Those words were still unspoken.

How she recalled the lack of feeling between them. There had not been any particular smiles, no laughter and certainly a sense of strain when it came to their conversation. Mayhap, she reflected, he had been in as much shock as she over their betrothal, which had led to a lack of affability. Whatever the reason, Marianne was anxious about his return, praying that he would, finally, propose to her. She could not imagine their betrothal coming to an end, knowing the anger that would fall on her were such a thing to occur. Her father would be furious and shame would be piled on her shoulders until she would be almost unable to withstand it. No, such a thing could never occur. The Viscount would *have* to propose very soon, surely, for the sake of both their families.

"We should return soon, my lady. You have been out overly long."

Hetty's voice was low, with only a hint of caution. Marianne glanced up at the cloudy sky, feeling the slight chill in the air as she realized that she had been out walking for a good deal longer than she had intended. Her thoughts had been entirely caught up with her betrothed, even though she had not ever intended to allow herself to think on him. Even now, she could almost *feel* his presence beside her, see the way his sharp hazel eyes glanced at her, holding an almost foreboding look. He was handsome, she had to admit, while turning back in the direction of her father's townhouse. Her stomach tightened as she let herself consider his features, thinking of his strong jaw, his dark brown hair which was always so carefully set in place. As yet, she had never seen him smile, recalling how his expression was always thoughtful yet rather severe, as though his thoughts were always at the forefront of his mind but yet never spoken. For a moment, Marianne wondered what Lord Galsworthy would look like should he allow those thoughts to be shared, if he allowed himself to truly be free with her. But the thought was dashed away in a moment. Lord Galsworthy had been distant and almost cold in the month they had already spent together, and she had no hope that he would be any different once he had returned from India.

Stepping inside, Marianne quickly removed her bonnet and gloves and handed them to the butler before dismissing Hetty. She had endured quite enough of Hetty's conversation for the time being and certainly did not want to have even another word exchanged with the maid for the moment. Marianne was just about to make her way up the stairs to the drawing room before the butler stopped her.

"My lady, you received a visitor this afternoon, but I informed him that you were not at home. He left a card and said that he would write a note requesting another day and time to call upon you."

Marianne, who had not been expecting anyone to call whilst she had been out for her daily walk, took the card with astonishment, looking at the inscription carefully. Her heart quickened for a moment, aware that this was the first gentleman who had ever sought her out in order to call upon her.

"Thank you," she murmured, glancing up at the butler. "Ensure that any note is brought to me directly."

"But of course," the butler replied, before carefully taking his leave of her. Marianne was left standing in the hallway, looking down at the card once more and wondering if this was what it felt like to truly have some sort of excitement over a particular gentleman's company. A smile crossed her face as she slipped the card into her pocket, making her way up the staircase in search of her sister. Even though in her heart, she knew that she ought not to be feeling any kind of eagerness over the visit of another gentleman who was not her betrothed, she tossed the thought aside. Marianne let her smile linger as she walked into the drawing room, telling herself that, in the end, it meant nothing at all.

CHAPTER THREE

"And how busy was town today?"

Marianne flopped into a chair, her smile fixed as she took in her younger sister, Harriet. Harriet had been busy reading a book by the fire until the moment Marianne had walked in and had now set the book down carefully by her side. Being the younger sister, she had enjoyed this year's London season without having any of the concerns that Marianne had over her betrothal.

"It was not particularly crowded," Marianne replied, quietly praying that Harriet would not begin to ask too many questions, not after she had just finished dealing with Hetty. "I confess that I did have to speak rather sharply to my maid."

Harriet lifted one eyebrow. "Oh?"

Sighing, Marianne waved a hand. "She was in a rather talkative mood, I confess," she replied, deciding not to talk about what Hetty had been discussing. "I was seeking some solitude for my thoughts."

Harriet laughed, the sound of her mirth bouncing off the walls and making Marianne smile. "If you wanted solitude, my dear sister, then you ought to have found your way into the library rather than step out of doors. The library is always quiet, as you know."

"I shall do so next time," Marianne promised sagely. "Are you enjoying your book?"

Unfortunately for Marianne, her sister was not quite finished with her questions, her blue eyes – so similar to Marianne's – narrowing just a little. "Never mind about my book," she began, tossing her head, her brown curls bouncing. "Why were you seeking solitude, Marianne?"

Closing her eyes, Marianne leaned back in her chair in a most unladylike fashion and shook her head. "I would rather not speak of it, Harriet."

"Oh, but you must!" Harriet exclaimed brightly. "It is much better to have such thoughts spoken aloud, is it not? Then they do not weigh on your mind as heavily as they have done before."

Marianne, who realized that she had been considering the very same thing about Lord Galsworthy, sighed heavily and opened her eyes. "Harriet, you need not pursue me with questions. There is nothing that weighs too heavily, I can assure you."

A knowing look crept into her sister's eyes. "This is about your betrothal, is it not? Lord Galsworthy is to return within the week, yes?"

Groaning inwardly, Marianne nodded slowly. "Yes, that is so, Harriet."

"You fear you will not be glad to see him again," Harriet murmured, appearing to be able to look into the depths of Marianne's mind and pull out her deepest fears.

Marianne sighed again. "Harriet, whether I am glad to see him again or not, I am resigned to the fact that I must wed him."

"I see," Harriet murmured, her book now entirely forgotten. "You fear that he will not be in any way pleased to be back in your company also?"

"I – I think I am a little concerned over this matter, yes," Marianne admitted quietly, feeling as though she was slowly pulling her heart apart in order to reveal her fears and worries to her sister and, whilst painful, finding it to be a somewhat cathartic exercise. "What if he shows no interest in my presence whatsoever, Harriet? It is not as though he was particularly eager in his courtship before he left for India."

Harriet, who was but three years younger than Marianne and had not yet found a suitable gentleman for herself, gave Marianne a sympathetic smile. "But Father says that he is a good match for you, Marianne."

"I am quite aware of that," Marianne replied with feeling, "but Father has never once considered matters of the heart when it comes to my marriage. I am quite sure that is because he has never had any sort of depth of feeling in his life, whether for Mama – God rest her – or for his daughters." She shook her head, her thoughts turning morose. "I have always prayed for some kind of fondness between myself and my future husband but, as things stand, Harriet, I know very little about Lord Galsworthy and certainly feel very little for him. I know that –"

"What is it that you feel, Marianne?"

Harriet had broken into Marianne's speech and was now looking at her with surprise flickering in her eyes. Not quite realizing what she had said, Marianne hesitated for a moment before coming to understand that she had expressed to her sister that there was some kind of feeling towards Lord Galsworthy that she had not yet admitted to Harriet.

"What I mean to say," she explained, a flush beginning to burn in her cheeks, "is that I feel nothing more than anxiety over his return. He did not show me any particular interest when he courted me and I fear that things will be much the same again."

There was a short pause. "Does this mean that you feel nothing for Lord Galsworthy, other than that?" Harriet asked, softly.

Marianne felt herself hesitate. "I –"

"Do you find him handsome?"

Marianne's flush increased all the more. "He is a handsome gentleman, yes, I will admit, but –"

"Does he have good conversation?"

A laugh escaped from Marianne. "I confess that we did not speak particularly often and when we did, it was somewhat stilted. I have wondered whether or not that was because he himself was also quite overcome with the news, although we never once discussed it."

Harriet smiled, a twinkle in her eye. "Well, at least you have been considering him," she murmured, catching Marianne's eye. "I think that you are quite afraid of what you yourself might feel when it comes to Lord Galsworthy, Marianne, should he turn out to be a gentleman of good character, which I am quite sure he is. After all, his mother speaks very highly of him."

Marianne laughed again, shaking her head. "Yes, but you quite forget that mothers have a tendency to speak well of their sons, regardless of their true character."

A slight shrug lifted Harriet's shoulders. "I suppose then you shall have to wait and see how he appears, Marianne. Why do you not speak to him openly about all that you feel?"

"Because we are not particularly close," Marianne replied quickly. "I cannot spread out my heart to him when we barely speak about anything of import."

Harriet tipped her head a little. "Well, if you truly wish for intimacy, if you truly wish to know his character, then you must pursue that through questions, through displaying the openness that you seek."

It was a thought, at least, and Marianne found herself not immediately able to respond. Even though Harriet was the younger, it often felt as though she had more wisdom and maturity than Marianne. It was as though, somehow, Harriet had been able to reveal to Marianne what she truly felt about Lord Galsworthy and the truth astonished her. She was not, as she had believed only a few minutes before, entirely closed to Lord Galsworthy. In all the letters she had written to him, in all the thoughts she'd had considering him, there had been something slowly growing deep within her. The fear that he would treat her as he had done before – as someone of little purpose who held very little interest for him – had blocked almost every other emotion, only for it to reveal itself to her at this very moment, sitting here in the drawing room opposite her sister.

"I will consider it," she promised softly, her gaze drifting away from Harriet as she looked, unseeingly, across the room.

"When do you expect him?" Harriet asked after a moment of silence. "Did he write to inform you?"

Marianne focused her eyes back onto her sister, clearing her throat as the flush faded from her cheeks. "His ship is due sometime this week, I think, but of course I have not heard from him since the week before he began his voyage."

Harriet nodded, no smile on her face. "Then you must prepare yourself, my dear sister. Consider what it is you want to say to him and how you are to greet him."

"Greet him?" Marianne repeated, a little bewildered.

"You must show him *some* affection, of course!" Harriet laughed as though she were talking to someone who had very little knowledge about the matter. "Regardless of whether you feel such a thing or not, you must show him that you are glad of his return. Ensure that he knows that the words you wrote at the end of each and every letter are true – that you *have* been eagerly awaiting his return and that you are truly delighted to have him back here in England. Hang onto his every word, smile brightly and press his hand if you can."

Marianne nodded, swallowing the lump that had quickly formed in her throat over the anxiety she felt at meeting him again. "I can attempt to do all of those things which you have suggested," she replied, seeing Harriet waiting for her response.

"I am quite sure that, once you show him such things, he will be quite unable to turn away from you. To return back to that distant, quiet gentleman he was before."

Marianne sighed heavily, pressing one hand to her heart. "I do hope so, Harriet," she admitted softly. "I fear that he will bring our betrothal to an end and never propose, as we are all expecting him to. What then? What am I to do then should he do so?"

Leaning forward, Harriet fixed her gaze onto Marianne, forcing away the sudden burst of panic which had shot through her. "You must not think such a thing, Marianne. A gentleman does not turn from such an obligation, especially not if it was of his father's doing."

Trying to reassure herself, Marianne smiled tightly. "I do hope so," she whispered, just as a rap at the door caught her attention. Turning, she called for them to enter, suddenly recalling the card in her pocket.

"My lady."

Hetty stepped inside and Marianne's smile quickly faded. "Yes, Hetty? What is it?"

"I heard some news from one of the errand boys that I thought I should tell you, my lady," Hetty said at once, sounding excited. "The ship, the one that Lord Galsworthy is on, it has been spotted off the coast of England."

Marianne's heart dropped to her toes, her breath catching. "'The Sea Maiden'?" she asked, seeing Harriet send a sharp glance in her direction.

"Yes, that be it, my lady," Hetty replied, looking thoroughly delighted. "They think it be but two days until it docks, if not sooner."

There was a sudden, strained silence as Marianne found her throat closing up, all sorts of emotions ripping through her as she tried her best to find something to say in response. The memory of how he had left her, bidding her farewell with a simple bow over her hand instead of any sort of affection, left her feeling suddenly cold.

"Thank you, Hetty," Harriet said, shattering the quiet. "As you can see, your mistress is overcome with the news." She sent a warning look in Marianne's direction who somehow managed to get her lips to curve into a semblance of a smile. The last thing she needed was for the staff to know that she felt anxious over her betrothed's return.

"I am," Marianne managed to say as Hetty's worried look faded away. "Quite overcome. Yes. Thank you for coming to inform me, Hetty."

Hetty nodded, bobbed, and inquired if there was anything else that they required. Sending her away with the direction that a tea tray be brought at once, Harriet let out a long breath and shook her head. "My dear Marianne, you must try to compose yourself, particularly in front of the staff."

"I am doing my best," Marianne replied, aware of just how quickly her heart was beating. "I am a little surprised, that is all."

Harriet shook her head in exasperation. "You knew he was to return soon, did you not? Now you must prepare yourself for his arrival, for I am quite certain that he will call upon you almost the moment he sets foot back in England."

Marianne did not feel the same certainty but tried to

smile, her heart pounding frantically as anxiety shot through her. "I do hope so, Harriet," she said softly, her fingers twisting together. "But I fear that he may avoid me altogether."

"Tosh!" Harriet exclaimed as Hetty arrived back with the tea tray. "He will be here taking tea with us both, very soon. I am quite sure of it."

CHAPTER FOUR

"Thank you, Captain, for a safe voyage."

The Captain chuckled, his beady eyes taking in Philip's dull countenance and rather unsteady footing.

"You have discovered, then, that the land is not as steady as it once seemed," he chuckled, putting a heavy hand on Philip's shoulder. "I did warn you, didn't I?"

Philip's lips twisted in a wry smile. "You did, Captain. Yes, it appears as though my legs are quite unused to walking on land again. I do hope their knowledge of steady ground will return soon." He tried to chuckle but the queasiness in his stomach doubled as he did so and so he immediately gave up the attempt.

"You will be yourself again by tomorrow," the Captain promised, making Philip let out a sigh of relief. "Thank you, my lord, for your kind gesture towards myself and my crew." He patted the pocket that now held the small bag of coins which Philip had given him, on top of the money owed for the journey. "Should you ever wish to return to India, I beg that you seek my ship out again."

"I will," Philip replied honestly. The man had captained the ship well and Philip had never once felt unsafe. "But I doubt that I shall return to India again in the next few years. I have plenty of responsibilities here." An image of Miss Weston flashed into his mind, his smile fading almost immediately. "Although I shall forever be grateful to you for bringing me here in safety."

They bade farewell and Philip immediately made his way to the carriage, knowing that it would not take him particularly long to return to his townhouse. He had no doubt that his mother would be waiting there, desperate to see him as she had claimed in her letters. Had it not been for his sister's presence here in London – for she had married one Lord Youngson only a few months before their father's death – then Philip might never have gone to India. His sister had assured him that she would care for their mother in the time he was away and so his mother's letters, begging him to return, had never truly worn upon his conscience.

You ought to go to see your bride.

Speaking of his conscience, the faint voice in his head now pricked at him uncomfortably, telling him that he ought to go to call upon Miss Weston at his earliest convenience. Grateful that the swaying of the carriage reminded him of the sea and, thus, took away some of his nausea, Philip closed his eyes and rested his head back against the squabs. He did not need to go and see the lady, he told himself, not immediately. He was still rather unsure on his feet, was he not, and certainly could not go into Lord Bridgestone's townhouse when he might cast up his accounts at any moment! No, he would need to wash, change, and rest before he allowed himself to call upon Miss Weston.

Opening his eyes, Philip allowed himself to look out of the carriage window, relieved that he did not immediately feel ill once more. It was very strange, being so aware that the thing he had longed for the most now felt so unusual to him. Solid ground had become the enemy to his stomach and his mind, making him feel so poorly that he wanted nothing other than to lie down and close his eyes. It reminded him of his first few days at sea, where he had clung to his bunk and inwardly cried out for respite. The Captain had assured him that it would pass – and so it had. Therefore, he had to pray that this strange feeling of sickness would wear off very soon. He had no doubt that his mother would nag at him about his duty to Miss Weston from almost the very moment he arrived home.

Home.

The word ought to have brought him joy, but instead, all he felt was an increasing dread. Home meant responsibility, it meant duty, and whilst he did not shirk from it, he did not wish to face it either. The things that were expected of him when it came to his estate were quite understandable and, as far as they were concerned, he both accepted and almost enjoyed them. But to marry and produce an heir was not something he truly felt prepared for. Especially when the betrothal had been foisted upon him, when he had not been given the opportunity to find a bride of his own. The shock of it had made him almost recoil, withdrawing into himself in the month he had been meant to be courting Miss Weston. To escape from her and from his duty had been his single aim, and he had done so quite wonderfully. To return to it now brought him no pleasure.

Suddenly, his breath caught. There! A face he recognized. He rapped on the roof, and the carriage came to a sudden halt, jerking him in his seat. Philip did not care. His gaze was entirely fixed on the lady walking towards Grosvenor Square.

It was Miss Weston.

She was more lovely than he remembered. The bonnet she wore did not quite manage to hide the curls which escaped from their confines, bouncing gently around her forehead as she attempted to push one back into its place. The gentle curve of her neck, her delicate cheekbones, the full, pink lips – how had he forgotten such beauty? The way her eyes roved all about her, filled with curiosity, as she took everyone and everything in, quite caught his interest. She was lovely in every which way. He ought to be delighted that such a beauty would be on his arm as his wife!

But there is more to a lady than her beauty.

Slowly, his heart began to settle from its wild, unsettling rhythm. He had allowed himself to be caught by her loveliness and had, at that moment, quite forgotten the rest of his difficulties when it came to considering her. There had been that uncertainty which had lingered on in his mind whenever he had thought of her these last few months. She had never appeared as free with him as she did now. There had never been that gentle smile curving her lips, that brightness in her eyes. He had been quite sure that it was because she did not wish to marry him, that her lack of willingness over their arranged betrothal had kept any sort of happiness from them both. Their lack of conversation, their absence of smiles and witty remarks had quite convinced him that she was more than reluctant to wed him. That was why, on seeing her now, Philip was quite sure she would never appear that way with him.

His gut twisted. Knocking on the roof again, he urged the carriage onwards, turning his face away from his bride to be. She had not seen him and that was probably for the best. He would have time to compose himself, to consider what he would say to her when they met again. Having now laid eyes on her, he would not be so caught by her beauty, would not be taken aback by the light in her eyes or the fair curls that brushed her temples. They would greet one another politely and he would do his duty as he had agreed.

Of course, he would still have to propose to her, as he had not yet managed to do. His brow furrowed as the carriage pulled up to his townhouse. Why was he so reluctant? It was the simplest of things and would set the wedding plans in motion, just as everyone expected. There would be the banns called and, after three Sundays, the marriage would take place. Thereafter, they would return to his estate and resume life there, as husband and wife.

Why, then, could he not find the courage to do such a simple thing as ask his betrothed to marry him? Regardless of what he felt, regardless of what he feared, it was his duty. And his duty was to marry Miss Weston.

"Oh, Galsworthy!"

Philip smiled tightly, spreading his hands. His mother, who had been sitting quietly in the drawing room with a tray by her side and a book in her hand had dropped the book in astonishment as he had entered and now had one hand pressed against her heart.

"You did not expect me, Mama?"

"Not until five days hence!" she exclaimed, not moving from her chair. "I thought to arrange a celebration for your return! It has all been arranged, Galsworthy! Why did you not write to tell me you were to return earlier than planned?"

Blowing out a slow breath of exasperation, Philip decided not to mention that he could not exactly write a letter and have it sent to his mother from the middle of the ocean.

"Well, we shall just have to continue on as planned," his mother continued, clearly unaware of the exasperation she was causing. "Five days, Galsworthy."

"Of course, Mama," Philip replied, a little disappointed at the welcome – or lack of it – that he had received from her. "I would not like to thwart your plans simply by appearing a little earlier than anticipated." His lips twisted in a wry smile, but his mother did not appear to notice.

"Your sister will have to be informed, and Youngson

too, of course," Lady Galsworthy continued, getting up from her chair with a deeply thoughtful expression on her face. "And Miss Weston too, of course." She shot him a sharp glance. "You have not been to see her as yet, have you?"

Philip shook his head. "No, Mama."

"It is just as well," his mother replied, surprising him. "You do have the air of the sea about you, Galsworthy." Wrinkling her nose, she cast him a slightly dark glance. "You will wash and change before you call upon her, of course."

"Of course, Mama," Philip agreed, firmly. "But I intend to rest first. Mayhap I shall call upon her tomorrow."

His mother gasped, one hand at her mouth. "Tomorrow, Galsworthy?" she asked hoarsely. "But you cannot, I –"

"She is to come to the celebration, yes?" Philip interrupted, growing more and more exasperated with his mother.

"Yes," his mother said, "Along with her father and sister, of course. But really, Galsworthy, you cannot –"

"Then I shall greet her there," Philip stated, somewhat glad of the excuse to delay the inevitable meeting further. He turned away and walked towards the door, tired of his mother's harsh words and her nagging which had begun practically the moment he had set foot in the house. All he wanted now was to relax in a warm bath before retiring to bed. He prayed that his sea legs would disappear for good by the time he arose. "Good evening,

Mama," he said firmly, before leaving the room and closing the door loudly behind him.

Some hours later, Philip found himself at Whites, an establishment he had not often frequented in his younger years. Having been a year away, and given that it was not the height of the Season, there were not many other patrons who he recognized.

On top of the fact that he was still feeling rather unwell, his growing discontent with his mother and his impending marriage had him feeling distinctly out of sorts, so he ensconced himself in a corner of the club, a good measure of whisky in his glass. This was better than remaining at home, knowing that his mother was displeased with his lack of interest in pursuing Miss Weston the moment he had returned to London. He did not want to marry and no amount of nagging and the like on her part would convince him to go to the lady.

"Is that you, Galsworthy?"

Philip looked up, surprised to see a gentleman he recognized coming towards him. He was tall and broad-shouldered, his clothing of the finest cut. Philip tried to place him, remembering his name just in time.

"Hilton?"

"Indeed," the gentleman replied, his smile widening as he looked at him. "Might I join you?"

Philip shrugged, but Lord Hilton seemed to take this as an invitation and came to sit beside him. This was not what he had wanted – conversation and the like – but it seemed that he was to have it regardless.

"So," Lord Hilton began, slapping Philip hard on the shoulder. "What is it that brings you to London at the very end of the Season? All the eligible young ladies are already gone from London if they are not engaged or wed!"

Philip snorted, eyeing Hilton carefully. "I have not come in search of a bride," he said bluntly, his stomach twisting at the very thought. He dared not tell Lord Hilton that he was, in fact, attempting to find the courage to even propose to the lady he was betrothed to.

Lord Hilton chuckled before throwing back his brandy and setting down his glass on the table, beckoning for a footman to bring him another. "No? I would have thought a gentleman such as yourself would have been considering finding yourself a suitable bride. In fact, given your absence this last year, I thought you might have found one and were courting her!"

"I have been in India, inspecting my father's – *my* – holdings there," Philip replied, hating that he had made such a mistake. "Having taken the title, I thought to look over my properties in their entirety."

Lord Hilton shrugged, making Philip feel as though he had explained himself unnecessarily. Heat crept into his face, but Lord Hilton did not appear to notice, now accepting his second brandy.

"I am a little surprised to hear *you* discussing matrimony when you yourself are not wed," Philip continued as Lord Hilton set his glass down. "From what I recall, you were not enamoured of the idea!" He suddenly recalled just how much of a rake Lord Hilton had been in the years Philip had been in London. The gentleman had never once considered settling down and had seemingly enjoyed having his way with as many ladies as he could. Of course, almost every young lady had fallen in love with Lord Hilton and he had broken every single heart.

"Ah," Lord Hilton chuckled, good-naturedly. "That is before I found myself hopelessly in love."

Philip jerked his head up, astonished.

"You are surprised, of course," Lord Hilton continued, laughing. "But it is quite true. Dear Miss Forthside, daughter to Viscount Stuart – Scottish, apparently – has quite captured my heart." He tipped his head and smiled, his eyes aglow with an emotion Philip did not quite understand. "We are to wed within the month."

Philip could not speak for a moment, quite overcome by this news. He had never once thought that Lord Hilton, whom he knew to be nothing more than a rake, would somehow be looking forward to matrimony! Such an emotion, such an evident joy, was something he could not understand.

"My – my congratulations," he muttered, lifting his glass in a half-attempt to toast Lord Hilton's happiness.

Lord Hilton grinned. "You are not at all inclined towards matrimony, then?" He chuckled, shaking his head. "I must hope that you can soon find the happiness that I have done, Galsworthy. All it takes is seeing the lady in question and your heart quite flies away!"

For a moment, a vision of Miss Weston sprang into Philip's mind, astonishing him. His whole body seemed to come to life in a single moment, his nausea dissipating as he thought of her.

And then, with an effort, he pushed it all away.

"I hardly think so," he replied somewhat coldly. "Although I wish you all the happiness in the world, Lord Hilton. I do not think it will be so for me." Rising from his chair, he ignored Lord Hilton's plea that he sit down and talk further, suddenly desperate to be alone. He did not want to think of Miss Weston, he did not want to consider matrimony, or even let his thoughts turn to the idea of love. It was not something he wanted to face, not something he even wanted to ponder at this present moment.

Praying that Gibbs, his long-suffering valet, who had weathered the journey to India and back rather better than he had himself, would have thought to put a full decanter of whisky or brandy into his bedchamber, Philip turned his feet in the direction of home. Hopefully, his mother would be abed and, with enough brandy flowing through his veins, he would be able to forget about Miss Weston and their betrothal entirely.

CHAPTER FIVE

"My lady?"

Marianne looked up from her book as her maid walked into the room, appearing a little confused.

"Yes, Hetty?" she asked, finding that she was a little frustrated with having been disturbed. The novel was rather exciting and it had distracted her from the fears and worries she felt over the imminent arrival of her betrothed.

"My lady, you have a gentleman here to see you," Hetty said quietly, closing the door firmly behind her. "In fact, he asks if you wish to take a short stroll with him about Grosvenor Square." A frown settled over her brow, making Marianne more than aware that her maid thoroughly disapproved.

"What is the gentleman's name?" she asked, setting her book aside.

"It is a Lord Henry Redmond, my lady," Hetty

answered, looking at Marianne with interest. "Have you been introduced to him before?"

Marianne considered for a moment before the memory of their introduction came to her. "Yes," she replied, getting to her feet with sudden, swift excitement. "Yes, I have been introduced. He is the heir to the Earl of Crompton. We danced at Lord Thornton's Ball and I believe he called upon me some two days ago, although I was not at home at the time." She remembered the card that he had left for her, recalling that he had stated that he would write to her in order to arrange another meeting. Apparently, he had chosen simply to appear at her father's door instead. The persistence of such attentions recommended him to her, although she had to take a moment to remind herself that she was betrothed to another.

"Is my father at home?" Marianne asked, looking up at her maid with a sudden, sharp look. If he was at home, then he would, most likely, be rather cross with her if she was to go out walking with a gentleman other than her betrothed. But if he were not at home, then she had nothing to concern herself about.

"No, he is not, my lady," Hetty replied slowly, her eyes flickering with concern. "He took your sister to afternoon tea with Lady Henstridge and her son, the soon to be Earl of Henstridge."

Quite aware that her father was keen to find a suitable match for her sister just as soon as Marianne herself was married, Marianne resisted the unladylike urge to roll her eyes. The silence that followed, however, was quite misinterpreted by the maid, who began to nod slowly.

"I will tell the gentleman that you are indisposed, of course," Hetty murmured, bobbing a curtsy. "Do excuse me, my lady."

"You shall do no such thing," Marianne exclaimed, angry at her maid's impertinence. "Hetty, you are forgetting your place."

Hetty, to her surprise, frowned and did not appear to be in any way sorry for her attitude. "I think, my lady, that to be seen out walking with another gentleman when you are soon to be publicly engaged is –"

"It is not a matter that you need concern yourself with, Hetty," Marianne interrupted briskly. "To walk with a gentleman means very little, given that there is no courtship or the like. Come now, go and prepare yourself to join us."

Hetty's frown did not disappear, but she did begrudgingly walk away from her mistress, leaving the door ajar as she did so. Marianne smiled to herself, smoothing down her gown with careful hands before making her way to the door. Lord Henry was not a gentleman she knew particularly well, but she had enjoyed the dance they had shared at the ball and she had found his conversation witty and delightful. To walk with him was simply that – a walk they would share together – and Marianne told herself, as she prepared herself, that she did not need to worry that anyone would think anything of it. London society was rife with gossipmongers and she knew full well that even a small indiscretion could ruin her pristine reputation, but this was nothing more than a short stroll in the cool September air. There were only a few smaller occasions during the autumn months before the little Season began in earnest. Whether she would be in London or at her husband's estate, Marianne did not know.

"Enough," she told her reflection, tucking in one errant curl underneath her bonnet before pulling on her gloves. "You need not overthink this, Marianne. Walk with Lord Henry and enjoy the afternoon air. You need not worry about anything else."

"My dear lady, you are quite a delight!"

Marianne found herself smiling despite herself, walking alongside Lord Henry as they made their way back to Grosvenor Square. "You are much too kind, my lord," she replied, looking up at him and seeing the way his green eyes sparkled with mirth.

"No, indeed not!" he exclaimed, waving his arm in an expansive gesture. "Indeed, I do not think that I can find the words to best express the delight that comes from being in your company."

"Now you are doing it much too brown, Lord Henry," Marianne replied, firmly, taking some of the sparkles from his eyes. "We are only just introduced and I fear that there is a good deal more to my character than you are aware. Why, I might be quite the most selfish, most arrogant creature you have ever met!"

Lord Henry did not appear to be turned away by this suggestion, the corner of his mouth tipped up with a smile. "Then I suppose I shall have to call upon you again, my lady, so that I can see whether or not this claim of a selfish nature is quite true."

Marianne's stomach dropped to her toes. She had been enjoying Lord Henry's company so much that she had quite forgotten about her betrothed. She could not allow another man to court her, not when Lord Galsworthy was to propose to her once he returned to England.

"This does not please you, I think," Lord Henry murmured, his expression now a little disappointed. "I am sorry."

"No," Marianne protested, turning towards him, and finding herself more confused than ever. "No, indeed not, Lord Henry. I confess that there is a good deal more to my situation that I am currently able to reveal at present."

"I see," Lord Henry replied with a look of under-standing. "You are promised to another?"

She swallowed hard, her words refusing to come to her lips. Marianne found that she could neither deny nor confirm that statement, struggling to know what to say when she herself was so uncertain.

"I will not pry," Lord Henry stammered, now looking quite embarrassed as he shifted from foot to foot, his face a little flushed. His eyes darted away from hers, his hands clasped behind his back as he cleared his throat. "I do apologize, my lady."

He took her hand and bowed over it. A little embar-rassed herself, Marianne pressed his hand for a moment as he bowed. "You need not apologize, Lord Henry," she stated, her heart quickening in a way it had never done with Lord Galsworthy. "It is I who ought to apologize. I am not making myself clear and that is only because my thoughts themselves are all twisted together." She gave him a warm yet rueful smile as he dropped her hand, stepping back quickly as he ought.

"Then, might I be permitted to call on you again, my lady?" he asked, his voice filled with hope as the air around them seemed to warm, taking away the chill from the wind that swept past them.

Marianne did not know what it was that made her say yes, but the word escaped from her mouth before she could prevent it. Lord Henry beamed with delight, bowed again, and took his leave, letting her climb the steps to her father's townhouse with Hetty just behind her.

Closing the door, Marianne handed her bonnet and gloves to the butler without a word, her brow furrowing as she considered what she had just agreed to. It had been a moment of foolishness, for she certainly could not agree to a gentleman courting her when she was betrothed to another. Her thoughts clouded. The depths of her fear told her that Lord Galsworthy would turn from her, that he would break their betrothal and leave her without hope. Where would she be then? Besides which, having such an attentive and conversational gentleman by her side had been a welcome happiness such as she had never experienced with Lord Galsworthy.

"My dear Marianne, where have you been?"

She looked up, torn from her thoughts as Harriet came rushing down the staircase towards her.

"I – I took a short walk," she stated as Hetty disappeared down the hallway, her back ramrod straight, displaying her stern dislike of Marianne's behaviour. Marianne ignored this and turned towards her sister, walking up the staircase towards her. Her stomach tightened with nerves, fearing that her father had seen her walking with Lord Henry as he had returned, and that Harriet was coming to warn her about his impending wrath.

"Oh, my dear sister, I have just heard the news from Miss Harestone! Why did you not tell me?" Harriet caught Marianne's hands and began to half drag her up the staircase. "When did he call? Was it when I was not at home yesterday evening? I am surprised, truly, that you did not say a word about it, not when you –"

"Harriet," Marianne interrupted, impatiently. "Of what are you speaking?"

Harriet stared at her for a moment, her mouth agape.

"I do not understand to whom you are referring," Marianne continued when her sister said nothing. "No-one has come to call."

"But – but he has been back in England for a day already," Harriet breathed, her eyes a little wide. "I thought that..." She trailed off, looking away from Marianne for a moment. "Well, I am quite sure he will call upon you very soon. After all, we are to go to his townhouse for the celebration in a few days."

"Celebration?"

"Yes, did Father not tell you?" Harriet exclaimed, looking as though Marianne was deliberately not understanding what she was saying. "Lady Galsworthy has arranged a celebration for Lord Galsworthy's return. It is to take place on Friday evening."

An ache began to burn in Marianne's mind. "Are you telling me, Harriet, that Lord Galsworthy has returned home to England?"

"Yes, that is exactly what I am saying," Harriet replied slowly. "I thought he would have called upon you almost the moment he came from the ship, but apparently he has not."

Marianne shook her head, her heart sinking towards the floor. "No," she said, numbly. "He has not called. Goodness, Harriet, I have not even received a note from him stating that he is safely returned!" Her eyes burned with sudden, sharp tears and her sister, on seeing this, pulled her quickly into the library so that none of the servants might hear their conversation.

"I am sure that he is simply tired from his journey," Harriet murmured as she pulled Marianne into a tight embrace. "Perhaps he wishes to ensure that he is entirely recovered before seeing you again. Mayhap he wishes to make the very best of impressions."

Marianne shook her head. "Or mayhap, my dear, he is quite unconcerned about me. I have no place in his thoughts from what I can see. It is just as I expected."

"No, surely not," Harriet replied gently, pressing Marianne's hands. "You are thinking much too poorly of him, my dear. Mayhap he is ill, mayhap he –"

"Being ill does not prevent one from writing a note to one's betrothed!" Marianne exclaimed, suddenly angry with Harriet's defense of him. "Being tired is no excuse either, surely! It is clear to me that he has no feelings towards me whatsoever. I am nothing more than a responsibility that must be fulfilled at some point, but he has no eagerness to do so." She shook her head, tears landing on her cheeks with some force as sobs began to rack her frame. All she had been feeling began to tear through her, all her fears and doubts suddenly bursting into life. She had listened to Harriet and allowed herself to feel some sort of hope that he might return to England with a greater depth of feeling for her than before, but it appeared that she had been quite mistaken. She certainly felt no guilt now in allowing Lord Henry to take her for a short stroll, nor for agreeing to allow him to call upon her again!

"I shall be nothing more than a neglected bride," she said, pulling her hands from Harriet. "*If* I wed him, of course."

Harriet looked astonished. "Of course you must marry him, Marianne. He is your betrothed!"

"And yet, I still have a choice, do I not?" Marianne asked tightly, dabbing at her cheeks with her lace handkerchief. "I know that Father would be greatly displeased and the *ton* would not be easily forgiving, but surely it is better to have the opportunity to find one's own husband than to be forced into a marriage such as this?" Her voice was rising steadily, her upset growing with every word she spoke. "No, Harriet, I will not simply agree to this marriage as I have done before. I have another –"

She stopped dead, realizing what it was she had been about to say. Her sister eyed her carefully, her cheeks a little pale.

"Do you mean to say you have another gentleman

caller?" Harriet asked softly, once a few moments of silence had passed. "Yes, I am aware that a gentleman has called here at the house in search of you but I had thought that you would have sent him away, given that you are betrothed."

Marianne lifted her chin and removed her gaze from her sister. "I have enjoyed his company very much," she replied steadily. "Besides which, Lord Galsworthy has not yet proposed, so I will not consider myself engaged. Not until such a thing occurs and I have accepted."

Harriet's face was now quite pale and she grasped Marianne's hand tightly, which Marianne both was grateful for and disliked in equal measure. Her sister could not understand, not really. She was not the one in Marianne's situation and was, therefore, able to study it without any sort of emotion. There was a detachment there that Marianne did not have. There was very little true understanding on Harriet's part, although Marianne was grateful that she was, at least, willing to listen to Marianne's tumultuous thoughts.

"You must be careful, Marianne."

Having expected Harriet to rail at her about her lack of consideration or appreciation for her betrothed, Marianne shot her sister a sharp look.

"I can see that you are deeply wounded by Lord Galsworthy's lack of attention to you," her sister said softly. "I have tried to understand his reasons for refusing to even send you a note announcing his arrival in town, but I cannot." Sighing heavily, she shook her head and let go of Marianne's hand. "If there is another gentleman who wishes to call upon you, then I cannot criticize your desire to accept him. I would only bid you to be more than careful, knowing that our father will be furious should he hear of it. He is not, after all, a gentleman with a good deal of understanding when it comes to matters of the heart."

Marianne gave her a wry smile. "No, he is not," she agreed. "I thank you, Harriet. I confess that I am greatly troubled by it all and yes, I am deeply wounded that my betrothed has not had the thought to send me even a note to speak of his return. That I had to find out the news from my sister, who heard it from someone entirely unrelated to us all!" Feeling tears threaten again, Marianne swallowed hard and turned her head away, blinking furiously. "It is quite thoughtless," she finished, her voice breaking just a little.

"It is," Harriet agreed, walking over to the bell pull and tugging it, evidently thinking that tea would bring a good deal of respite to Marianne's present troubles. "And might I ask the name of the gentleman who has come to call upon you?"

Marianne felt a warm glow rise up in her heart as she thought of how they had laughed and talked that afternoon. He had been almost everything she had been hoping for with Lord Galsworthy, and certainly, he was a good deal more considerate! "Lord Henry Redmond," she replied with a small smile tugging at her lips. "He is rather persistent in his attentions, which I will not fault him for. It is a wonderful thing to be so desired, Harriet."

A warning climbed into Harriet's expression but, to Marianne's relief, she kept her mouth closed tightly.

"I did tell him that he could call again," Marianne

confessed, seeing Harriet nod. "At the time I felt as though I were being unfair and quite rude to Lord Galsworthy, but now..." She shook her head to herself, feeling her resolve growing steadily. "Now, I feel as though I am quite absolved of all guilt. Should he come to call again, I will welcome his attentions and will not turn from them."

"Just so long as our father does not find out his intentions," Harriet reminded her darkly. "Else I fear it all may come tumbling around your ears."

Marianne shrugged, trying to remain as nonchalant as she could. "He will not," she replied airily. "I will be just as he expects of me when it comes to speaking with Lord Galsworthy. He will find no fault with me, I am quite sure."

"I do hope so," Harriet replied just as the door opened to reveal a maid with a tea tray held in her hands. "I cannot imagine what would happen should Lord Galsworthy hear that you are being courted by another!"

The thought caught Marianne's mind and she held it there for a moment, choosing to let her thoughts linger on the notion. What would Lord Galsworthy do should he find out that she was the sole focus of another gentleman's attentions? Would it rouse his passions, force him to actually *feel* something for her, other than clear disinterest? Or would he, as she expected, simply shrug, and turn away, not particularly interested in her or her actions?

"We will see," Marianne murmured to herself as Harriet began to pour the tea. Tomorrow's dinner with Lord Galsworthy would certainly be interesting, although Marianne was glad that, even if her betrothed said nothing more than a few words to her, she would have the knowledge that another gentleman thought her both interesting and witty. Another gentleman wanted her company and her time. Another gentleman showed her more consideration than her own betrothed and, mayhap in time, he would become more to her than Lord Galsworthy ever could.

CHAPTER SIX

Having been desperate to escape from yet another of his mother's speeches about how terrible a gentleman he was for not calling upon his betrothed almost the moment he had set foot on shore, Philip had chosen to step out of doors this afternoon.

He did not exactly relish the idea of being out in the fresh air, given that he would much rather have been in bed, or at the very least, spending a quiet afternoon in his study getting himself reacquainted with all of his current responsibilities. However, knowing that his mother would be constantly at his arm, haranguing him until, most likely, he decided to do as she asked, he had braved the outdoors.

Sighing heavily to himself, Philip lengthened his stride and strode quickly towards St. James' Park, praying that the hour was early enough for the usual patrons not to be present as yet. The last thing he wanted was prolonged conversation, not when his mind was already busy with a great many thoughts, most of them centered around his betrothed. It was, of course, quite unreasonable that he had not as yet called upon her, had not yet even written to her to announce his return to England, but it was as though he did not wish to accept that part of his life again. Not until he absolutely had to. Unfortunately, the more his mother chased him to call upon Miss Weston, the more he was absolutely determined not to do so.

Suddenly overcome by a stab of guilt, Philip stopped dead in his tracks and put one hand over his eyes. Goodness, was this what he had become? Selfish, stubborn, and prideful? He had not once thought about how Miss Weston would be feeling over his current lack of interest towards her, attempting to convince himself that she did not much care for him regardless. It was entirely unfair of him to behave in such a way. He was not a coward, he was not a cruel man. No, he would have to put aside his own selfish feelings and do as he ought, out of consideration for her.

"You look as though you are in the depths of despair."

A familiar voice caught Philip by surprise and he looked up to see none other than Lord Hilton, who was walking alongside a beautiful young lady whom Philip presumed to be Miss Forthside, Lord Hilton's betrothed. What astonished him all the more was just how delighted Lord Hilton appeared to be as he drew nearer to Philip, looking down fondly at the lady on his arm. Miss Forthside had eyes only for her betrothed, blushing furiously at something the gentleman said to her as they drew near.

"Lord Hilton," Philip murmured, suddenly struck by a pang of longing that quite startled him. "And this must be Miss Forthside." He swept into a bow as the lady greeted him. "How delightful to meet you."

"Isn't she just wonderful?" Lord Hilton murmured as Miss Forthside smiled and lowered her eyes demurely. "You have not found yourself engaged since I last saw you, Galsworthy? It is the most capital state. I do hope the pain I saw on your face but a moment ago is not because of a broken heart."

Philip snorted, only just managing to stop himself from rolling his eyes. "Given that I only saw you but two days ago, Lord Hilton, I hardly think that is anywhere near enough time to procure a bride."

Lord Hilton grinned good-naturedly. "Well, one never can tell when the first flurry of love might strike, Lord Galsworthy." He continued on, talking in depth about just how differently he felt, and Philip found himself staring at the gentleman in complete astonishment. Was this really the very same Lord Hilton? Could it be that he had been so changed simply by falling in love with a lady such as Miss Forthside? It was completely perplexing to Philip, given that he had only felt a very faint stirring when it came to Miss Weston and even that he had tried to ignore.

"Might you like to walk with us for a time, Lord Galsworthy?" Miss Forthside asked in her gentle Scottish lilt. "The park is not yet busy, although I can see a few carriages have arrived."

Philip turned to survey the scene, seeing that three carriages had now entered the park. He was about to thank them and explain that he was quite content in his own company and would not want to intrude upon their time together, when something – or, as it was, someone – caught his eye.

It was Miss Weston.

The carriages were, of course, being driven rather slowly around the park, to give the occupants within the best view of those out walking, which meant that Philip could clearly see Miss Weston sitting within one of those carriages, her eyes bright with laughter and a wide smile on her face.

His heart turned over within his chest.

A gentleman sat opposite her, looking out across the park and, Miss Harriet Weston sat beside her. He did not know the gentleman. Beside the man, looking most uncomfortable, sat Miss Weston's maid, apparently as chaperone.

Miss Weston was talking and laughing with the gentleman Philip did not know, and Philip found that his hands had slowly begun to curl into fists, for whatever reason. He was angry, he discovered, although he was not quite certain why. It appeared that the gentleman in question was simply taking both the Misses Weston out for a drive and, most likely, he was hoping to court Miss Harriet Weston and her sister, therefore, was accompanying them both. That was the most reasonable explanation, but still, Philip could not find it within himself to be rational. The urge to stop the carriage and demand his betrothed descend and walk with him was almost overwhelming. It was to the point that Philip found himself starting forward, only to stop himself dead with an effort.

"My, my," Lord Hilton remarked with an interested

look on his face. "You are quite het up about something, are you not?"

Philip, who had quite forgotten that he was with company, turned his head away from the carriage with an effort. "I thought I saw... someone," he stammered, trying to push the image of Miss Weston from his mind. "It is not at all important."

Lord Hilton chuckled and threw a knowing glance towards Miss Forthside, who returned it with a smile. "I will not accept that as an answer, Galsworthy. I can see that you are upset about something, perhaps even jealous?"

"Not in the least!" Philip exclaimed, feeling heat rise in his face as he tried to ignore the carriage completely, seeing that it was turning towards the path where they now stood. "Do excuse me, Hilton, Miss Forthside. I have just remembered a matter of business which I must see to at this very moment. Do excuse me."

"Of course," Lord Hilton replied, his smile never slipping. "Although I do hope that one day soon you will be able to reveal to me just who it is that is causing you such distress."

Philip bowed to Miss Forthside, who bid him farewell, managing to hold his tongue as he did so. The urge to argue with Lord Hilton was very strong, but seeing that the carriage itself was now drawing nearer, Philip was forced to retreat. He did not want to greet his betrothed here, not in the park in front of Lord Hilton and whoever it was in the carriage. It would be too obvious to them all that something of import was between himself and Miss Weston. Besides which, he was much too angry to deal with the situation as it now stood. He would have to think things over carefully and allow himself time to consider the matter calmly. For the moment, he was much too on edge to even greet the lady.

Turning towards home, Philip hastened towards the gate of the park, his mind heavy with thoughts. Why had he reacted so strongly to seeing Miss Weston with another gentleman, when it was quite obvious that she was simply accompanying her sister? Why had he found himself so furious? Was there even the slightest chance that he was, as Lord Hilton had implied, jealous of the gentleman? That would mean, of course, that he felt more for the lady than he wanted to admit.

Shaking his head to himself, Philip muttered darkly under his breath as he stalked home. Sometimes he wished he had never returned to England at all.

"My lord?"

Philip lifted his head from the pillows and groaned, feeling the bright morning sun pierce his eyes as the curtains were drawn back – most likely, at the behest of his mother. Having drunk far too much brandy last evening, he now felt the full effects of it all through him. His head was in agony.

"I shall set your breakfast tray just by the fire, my lord," his valet continued when Philip said nothing. "It is a fine day, my lord, a fine day."

"I am glad to hear it," Philip muttered under his

breath, not feeling at all the thing. "Do be off with you now. I am still quite exhausted."

Gibbs, however, simply cleared his throat, placed his hand behind his back and remained exactly where he was as the footman continued to bustle about in Philip's room, tying back the curtains and building up the fire in the grate so that it might be warm enough for Philip to dress.

Closing his eyes again, Philip sighed heavily to himself. "Close the drapes. The light pains my eyes."

He waited until his orders had been carried out before directing his tired eyes back towards his valet. "What is it?"

Gibbs cleared his throat again. "My lord, Lady Galsworthy bid me to inform you that tonight is the evening of the celebration of your return."

"Yes," Philip replied firmly. "I am aware of it." Even though he had been away from the sea for some days, his legs still certainly did not feel as though they appreciated being back on England's shores. He had retired to bed early last evening, still feeling rotten whilst the voice of his mother had floated up the stairs behind him, railing at him for leaving her side when she had no other company to speak of. It was not as though he had not ensured that he had remained with her all through dinner, instead of taking a tray in his room, but that had not been enough for her. She had wanted to talk in depth about all that was planned for this supposedly wonderful celebration, whereas all he had wanted to do was to lie down in his dark room and close his eyes. Of course, the moment he had done so, thoughts of Miss Weston and the gentleman in the carriage had begun to assail him and so, in desperation, he had turned to the brandy.

He had to pray that this morning would allow him to feel a little better, once he found the energy required to rise from his bed.

"My lord," Gibbs continued, now appearing rather awkward. "Your mother also bade me inform you that your betrothed is residing at home for the remainder of the day, should you wish to call."

Philip's eyes shot open and he saw Gibbs' cheeks flush with color, evidently mortified that he had been forced to make such a statement, but having had little choice in the matter. Philip, knowing just how tyrannical his mother could be at times, chose not to say a single word, dismissing Gibbs with a wave of his hand.

"Please allow me some time to eat, then return to assist me with dressing."

"Thank you, my lord." Gibbs bowed deeply, evidently quite relieved that he was not to be railed at for bringing such a message to Philip. Leaving the room, he pulled the door closed tightly and left Philip in peace.

Groaning, Philip threw his head back against the pillows and squeezed his eyes shut tightly. He did not want his mother's interference and certainly could not allow her to tell him what he ought to be doing when it came to his betrothed! He had no particular wish to call upon Miss Weston, given that she was to be attending the celebration this evening, but he was quite sure his mother had either promised the girl or had made the suggestion that he would do just that. Not that he knew when his mother would have seen Miss Weston, but it was just the sort of thing that his mother would do. She was doing her best to improve the situation between them and Philip did not appreciate her efforts. The fact that he had not written to Miss Weston to inform her that he had returned was, as he now understood, something of an insult. Although, he had made the excuse to himself that the lady would understand that he had been recovering from his travels and had not wished to inform her that he was home without being able to call upon her in person. Unfortunately, he knew full well that he had not written to her, despite his realization that he was being something of an oaf, because he was struggling with what he had seen and the emotions that had risen in him at the sight of it.

However, knowing that she was to be at his home this evening was more than enough to deal with for the moment, for he had to confront the fact that he was just as unwilling to marry as he had been before he'd left for India. Yes, she was beautiful and that was, he supposed, a piece of good fortune, but to settle down, bear children and continue as a married man without any sort of feeling between them felt more like a punishment than any sort of blessing. Why could he not have her smile at him as she had done to the gentleman in the carriage? Why had there never been anything but awkwardness and tension between them? And what if he began to feel something deep and true for her, but she felt nothing in return? What agonies would that bring?

"You will do your duty."

Those words were spoken from his lips without him even thinking them. His mother had repeated that over and over ever since he had returned home, as though she knew that he was considering his future with a good deal of severity. It was not as though he was entirely unaware of what his duty was, nor that he ought to be pursuing it with an eager intent, but he simply could not rouse such feelings within himself.

Throwing back the covers, Philip rose unsteadily, feeling his legs a little weak but certainly a good deal better than last evening when he had been required to force one foot in front of the other simply to climb the staircase to his bedchamber. Who would have thought that traveling by ship would make one so weary and so ill for such a prolonged length of time? *Although you did not exactly help matters by your indulgence in the finest French brandy,* he thought to himself, his head swimming.

Closing his eyes again as he sat down in a chair by the fire, Philip settled his head into his hands for a moment, knowing just how little he was excited about this evening's events. To have to converse with everyone, to have people throwing knowing looks his way, to have the expectation that he would propose to Miss Weston very soon all bit at him painfully. He did not want to have to act and pretend, like some foolish court jester with a painted smile on their face. To appear delighted to be back in England, to appear as though he could think of nothing more wonderful than marrying and begetting an heir was all more than Philip thought he could bear. What made it all the worse was knowing that Miss Weston would be doing as much play-acting as he. There would be a ready smile that would not quite reach her eyes, a brightness in her expression that would fade the moment she turned away.

"Galsworthy?"

Groaning, Philip wished to goodness he had thought to lock his bedchamber door, for it was his mother's shrill voice coming from the other side.

"Do ensure you are dressed, my boy, for I have something I wish to say to you."

Philip, knowing that he could not exactly prevent his mother from doing just as she pleased, begged her to wait for a moment before quickly drawing on a pair of pantaloons and tying his robe a good deal more tightly about his waist as though it were some kind of protection against his mother's sharp words. The moment he called for her to enter, the door opened and she walked in, sitting down opposite him with a glint in her eye that told him there was a storm growing steadily. Evidently, his response to Gibbs with regards to calling upon Miss Weston had not been good enough.

"Yes, Mama?" he asked, resigned to the fact that she was about to drag him across hot coals for failing to do as she wished.

"My dear boy, why is it that you do not wish to call upon your betrothed?"

This was not quite what he had been expecting, and he felt himself tense just a little as he looked back at her. There was a frown forming between her brows and her eyes were no longer hard and cold, but rather slowly filling with a concern he had not seen before.

"Mama," he began haltingly. "It is just that... I find

that I – I am quite content with the thought of seeing her this evening."

Her frown deepened. "Have you written to her, in order to inform her of your return?"

Shaking his head, he lifted one shoulder. "As I said, I will see her this evening, Mama.

"But she will be snubbed!" his mother exclaimed, sounding horrified. "She will think you care nothing for her, Galsworthy!"

"And I do not."

The words slipped from his mouth before he could prevent them. Snapping his mouth closed, he dropped his gaze and stared mutely at the floor. His mother said nothing for some minutes, the air growing thick with strain and tension.

"Oh, Galsworthy," she said eventually, heaving a great sigh. "Your absence has affected you in more ways than I expected. I am quite sure that when you see her again, you will be caught up with delight over her."

It was now Philip's turn to sigh, one hand rubbing his forehead as he did so. "I doubt that, Mama. You forget that this betrothal was simply handed to me, as though it were something I ought to be pleased with. I have never had the opportunity to seek out a lady of my own choosing. It is as though you expect myself and Miss Weston to simply rub along well together, without any particular difficulty." He raised his eyebrows, seeing his mother's surprise. "Did you think that I was truly pleased with such an arrangement, Mama? I have accepted it because I have no other choice, but I am not delighted by it, no. I will marry the girl because that is what duty requires of me, but I do not go into it with a heart filled with joy and contentment." He did not speak of what he had felt for the lady on seeing her with another gentleman and certainly made no mention of the fact that he had even seen her at all, for his mother would simply hold onto that fact and question him all the more fervently.

His words bounced around the room long after he was finished speaking, repeating themselves over and over as he lowered his head into his hands, quite certain that his mother would have more than enough to say in response to his complaint. For a long time, however, she was quite silent. They sat in the room as though made of marble, their gazes focused yet unfixed. Eventually, Philip sat up and regarded his mother carefully, seeing the astonishment that had come into her expression.

"You have never once expressed any sort of discontent," she whispered when he lifted one eyebrow.

"I know my responsibilities," he replied gruffly. "Do you truly believe that I could turn from my own father's will? He arranged my betrothal before he passed away and, given that Miss Weston's father had agreed wholeheartedly to the match, it was not as though I could refuse." Bitterness laced his words and he turned his head away from her, pain slicing through his heart. "I am aware that my father wanted what was best for me, as he saw it, and therefore I am doing my duty," he finished numbly. "Do not ask any more of me, Mama. Do not ask me to be joyful or delighted, or any other emotion that I must pretend to wear. It is not in me to do so."

After a few more minutes of silence, his mother rose

from her chair and, as she passed him, put one hand lightly on his shoulder.

"My dear son," she said with a good deal more gentleness than he had expected from her. "I have always wanted the best for you. I have high expectations for you and you have never once neglected to fulfill them. However, it appears that there is a lack of openness between us and for that I am truly sorry."

Looking up at her in surprise, Philip saw his mother's sadness and felt his heart wrench. The truth was, he had often longed for a closer acquaintance with his mother but, even as he had returned home to England, he had braced himself for the harsh words and the criticism that would undoubtedly come his way.

"I have not been the kindest of mothers, have I?" Lady Galsworthy continued, her voice quiet and tremulous as her gaze drifted away from him. "I have been unbending, unflinching and unkind." Her lips trembled, tears filling her eyes, and Philip felt his heart break asunder, even though he could find nothing to say that would refute all that his mother said. It was quite true. Every word of it.

"I am astonished to hear that you are so unsure of your betrothed," she said hoarsely. "You have never spoken to me of such a thing before, Galsworthy, but I do not blame you for that. It is I who is at fault for never encouraging you to speak with openness and honesty. There is a good deal I must reflect on."

"I did not mean to wound you, Mama."

A tight smile crossed her face, a single tear trickling down her worn cheek. "You have not," she replied quietly. "This is not your doing, Galsworthy. It is as though I have only just seen myself as I truly am, as though I have only just now noticed the knife which I placed in my heart so long ago." Her hand tightened on his shoulder before she let go entirely. "I must go."

Philip watched her leave, feeling entirely helpless and yet almost relieved that they had been able to have such a conversation. It was not as if he was glad to see his mother so upset, but glad for that the freedom with which they had both spoken. His mother was quite correct to say that he had never spoken to her with such honesty before and, now that he had, it appeared to have revealed a great many things to her, as well as to himself.

Perhaps there was more to his mother than he knew. Mayhap, underneath her sternness and harsh words, there was a heart which was filled with affection for him. This had been her way, perhaps, of seeing he had the best in life, that he would have a wife and family with which to surround himself and carry on the family line. He had always thought she cared for nothing more than duty and honor, but mayhap he had been mistaken in such a thing. For someone to change so quickly, so drastically, had quite taken his breath away.

It was not as though he needed his mother's permission to bring an end to his betrothal, but the thought had never really come into his mind with any degree of true consideration, given the shame and the pain that it would bring. Now, however, he realized that his mother might be a little more open to the idea, as she knew how he truly felt about the matter.

"No," he said aloud, his eyes turning to the breakfast

tray as he tried to put all such thoughts from his mind. "No, I have given my word and I will see it is done." He could not turn from the lady – or his mother – now, given that he had promised to marry Miss Weston. Whether he wanted to do so or not, Philip was not about to break his word, for to do so would be quite unconscionable. His word was entwined with his honour and he would not bring shame to his name by doing such a thing.

"Then you shall meet her this evening and do all that is expected," he told himself, pouring now lukewarm coffee into his china cup. He drank it anyway, his heart filled with all sorts of questions, surrounded by a great many swirling emotions. He felt as though he might come apart at the seams, quite overwhelmed by everything that had just occurred and all that would occur later that evening.

Once you propose to her, then you will be a good deal more settled.

Gritting his teeth, Philip tried to find the determination to do such a thing that very evening, but try as he might, his reluctance continued to pull him back. No matter what he did, not matter how hard he tried, he simply could not find the desire he needed to propose to the lady. It seemed he was to be in torment for a little longer.

CHAPTER SEVEN

"My dear Miss Weston!"

Philip's stomach twisted itself in knots as he saw his bride-to-be enter the drawing room with her father by her side. She did not look at him but greeted his mother with grace and elegance. She enquired after Lady Galsworthy's health and, having been assured that the lady was doing wonderfully, stepped forward to greet Philip.

Still, she did not look at him. Philip cleared his throat and took her hand in his, bowing over it as he was expected to do. "Miss Weston," he said in a voice that was a little too hoarse for his liking. "How very good to see you again."

She smiled tightly. "I hear you have been back in London for some days, my lord."

There was a veil covering her words and, attempting to draw it aside, Philip found himself able to discover a small hint of anger behind it. "Yes, Miss Weston," he replied, his heart hammering in his chest as he spoke.

"Unfortunately, I have been rather unwell. Becoming used to dry land again takes a little more time than I expected." It was not the entirety of the truth, but it would do.

There was a moment of silence. Throwing a sidelong glance towards his mother, Philip saw that she was busy conversing with Lord Bridgestone, Miss Weston's father. It was quite purposeful, he was sure, so that he would have ample opportunity to speak to Miss Weston. Her sister, Miss Harriet Weston, was also standing a little further away, although her sharp eyes lingered on them both without any sense of shame at doing so.

"I see," Miss Weston replied, her gaze finally settling on his. Philip found her eyes to be as cool as the sea on a rough, stormy day, the ice in them beginning to freeze his heart. "You must have been terribly ill if you could not so much as rouse yourself in order to pen a short note to your betrothed."

He swallowed hard, seeing the reason for her upset and yet finding the way that she was directing it towards him to be both insincere and foolish. "If you are filled with discontent that I did not write to you the very moment I came to shore, then you may be honest with me, Miss Weston," he replied firmly. "Perhaps it is for the best that we are both honest with one another, since I feel that very little of such a thing has ever passed between us. If I am to tell you the truth, my lady, it is that I was not certain of the reception I would be given from you. I have had several things on my mind of late and some have taken a good deal of getting used to." *Even the fact that, as I held your hand in mine, my heart quickened a little.*

Something changed in her expression, although she said nothing. He could not quite make out what it was, although there certainly was an astonishment that he had spoken to her so directly.

"Why do you not talk with Miss Weston out on the terrace?"

He turned his head to see Lord Bridgestone beaming at them both, evidently delighted with his rather impertinent suggestion. After taking a moment to regain his composure, aware of how Miss Marianne Weston and Miss Harriet Weston were both blushing furiously with the shame of what their father had said, he turned back to his betrothed.

"Of course, Miss Weston. How foolish of me to keep you here when we might talk with a little more privacy out on the terrace," he said with a small smile that did not betray his frustration. "Might you wish to join me?" Holding out his arm to her, he did not miss the way she hesitated for a moment before accepting it. Of course, given that both their families knew of their betrothal, there was no great surprise at this from either his mother or Miss Weston's sister, but Philip was all too aware of the other guests who, as yet, did not know of their arrangement.

The terrace was quiet and he felt Miss Weston's hand fall from his arm almost the moment they reached it. The door was still wide open and a few other guests came and went, all laughing and talking as they did so. He and Miss Weston stood to one side of the terrace, half hidden in shadow. Miss Weston looked directly ahead of her, her expression set hard. Philip found himself in the usual position of not knowing what to say to the lady, realizing that he had, after a moment of honesty, retreated back into himself, to how he had been before. This was how he had behaved with her before he left for India – quiet, reserved and entirely boring. Whether or not he had the desire to marry her, Philip knew that he would have to make more of an effort to converse with the lady, to know her better so that he might find the courage to propose and start the wedding plans.

"How was your time in India, my lord?"

She had not looked at him but he found himself grateful for it, given that he felt a good deal less ill at ease when she was looking away from him. "It was productive," he replied, with a small shrug.

"I was grateful for your letters," she continued, her voice soft, her words no longer bearing the hard edge that it had once done. "I do hope you found some enjoyment in my correspondence."

"Of course."

The agreement came from him without hesitation and, at that moment, Philip realized that yes, he had been quite glad of the letters. He had not realized it before now, looking back on his time in India with a perspective which was slightly different from how he had considered it during his time there.

"Truly, Lord Galsworthy?" Miss Weston turned to face him now, her face pale in the moonlight, and he was struck again by just how very lovely she was. Uncertainty laced her words and he found himself nodding fervently, eager to prove to her that he had truly been glad of them.

"Your questions were always of interest to me," he

said honestly. "I was glad to receive each letter, although I apologize that I did not always reply to you with the frequency you deserved."

A small smile tugged at her lips and, with that, Philip felt himself relax just a little. For the next few minutes, their conversation flowed with a good deal more ease than he had expected and he found himself beginning to enjoy what they spoke of. There was a growing sense of effortlessness as they spoke and Miss Weston herself appeared to be a good deal more open than before. This was not the lady he remembered, surely? When they had parted, he had felt relief in leaving the doubt-ridden Miss Weston behind, but now she appeared to have a good deal more strength within herself, as though she had made the decision to simply get on with things as she was expected to do. Perhaps, he thought to himself, as she laughed at something he said, there was more to Miss Weston than he had allowed himself to believe. Mayhap, once the uncertainty and confusion had dissipated from her, there might be a friendship which could grow between them. He might be able to actually enjoy her company, instead of fearing that there would be nothing between them for the rest of their days. As they continued to converse, as she continued to smile, Philip felt his heart begin to release itself from its confines of doubt and frustration, a warmth beginning to spread through it as he regarded her. She was, he realized, witty and bright, with good conversation and an elegance that brought him nothing but delight. Why had he not seen in her such a light before?

"I am truly sorry I did not write to you the very

moment I returned to England," he said truthfully, seeing her smile begin to fade away. "Miss Weston, I will confess that I have been the most selfish gentleman these last few days. I have thought nothing of others, putting my own health and my own requirements before anything else." Looking up at her, he felt a stab of guilt. "Even you, Miss Weston. That was quite wrong of me, I confess. Might you be willing to forgive me?"

There was a moment or two of complete silence. Miss Weston was looking back at him steadily, although her face was shuttered so that he could not read her expression. He could not know what she was thinking, finding himself growing more and more anxious as the moments passed.

"I think, my lord, that I have very little choice in the matter," she said eventually, her gaze drifting away from him. "After all, we are to marry and one cannot exactly hold a grudge against one's husband." The corner of her mouth quirked and a wave of relief crashed all through him.

"Indeed not," he replied, one hand at his heart as he gave her a short bow. "Thank you, Miss Weston. You are very kind."

"This honesty you speak of, my lord," she continued the moment he lifted his head. "I confess that I feel this has long been lacking in our... acquaintance. Even though you have been in India and I lingering here in England, neither of us have ever truly been open with the other, not even in our correspondence. Would you agree?"

He nodded. "I would," he stated without the slightest hesitation. "I confess that I had not thought to be so with anyone of my acquaintance, but after a conversation with my dear mother earlier today..." He trailed off, caught up with his thoughts as he recalled just how upset his mother had been at his confession. Glancing up, he saw Miss Weston looking back at him with a good deal of interest on her face, waiting for him to continue. Feeling heat ripple up his neck and into his cheeks, he cleared his throat and clasped his hands behind his back, knowing that to be open and honest with her would require a good deal of vulnerability on his part, a vulnerability he was not at all used to. He could not tell her of the jealousy he had felt upon seeing her with another gentleman, not yet. It was all too new to him, too strange an emotion. At the very least, however, he could tell her what it was he wished for them both to be to one another. That honesty would not reveal too much of himself as yet. It would take time for them both to be open with one another, he realized, even though it was he himself who wished to be closer. "What I am trying to say, Miss Weston, is that I do not want to remain strangers. I am tired of pretending."

A frown caught her brow. "Pretending?" she replied, looking a little confused.

It was not something he wanted to explain, realizing that he did not need to express to her how much he had despised the thought of marrying a lady he did not know and certainly did not care for, given that it would only injure her. All that was required was that he attempt to be a good deal more honest with the lady from this day forward. "That does not matter," he said, waving a hand. "What I hope for, Miss Weston, is that we might develop our acquaintance further with every day that passes. I confess that the betrothal was rather a shock to me, but that I am resigned to it now. I –"

"*Resigned* to it?"

Miss Weston's voice had become hard and Philip caught his breath, realizing what he had said.

"Miss Weston," he began, stammering as he tried to find some way to explain what he meant. "You must understand. I –"

"I quite understand," Miss Weston interrupted, her back stiff and eyes blazing. "You have decided to be truthful with me, Lord Galsworthy, and so the words of truth have come from your lips. You are not in any way pleased about our union and therefore are making as little effort as possible with our acquaintance. You speak of honesty, but it is only to wound me. Your words prove to me what I have long thought – that you do not wish to marry me, that you care nothing for me and have decided to make no considerable effort to further our acquaintance, to know my character and my heart." Her eyes flooded with tears and Philip felt himself flush with embarrassment. Somehow, he had managed to make a cake of himself and, worse still, had brought Miss Weston pain.

"Do excuse me, Lord Galsworthy," she finished, stepping past him. "I find that our conversation and your truthful words no longer bring me any sort of joy."

"Please, Miss Weston, wait!" he exclaimed, reaching for her arm. "That is not what I meant to say. I mean, it is, but that is not how things shall always be, I am quite sure of it. I do not know you as I intend to. The furthering of our acquaintance will quite change my attitude, I am certain of it!"

You have made things all the worse.

Closing his eyes, Philip let his hand drop from her arm, aware of how she was looking at him. There was a sadness and an agony in her eyes that he could not bear to see.

"If that is the case, my lord," she replied in a voice broken by deep, painful emotion, "if that is truly what you feel, then I expect your public proposal to occur very soon, so that we might begin preparations for our wedding day. Else I shall know that you are still as *resigned* to your fate as you have always been. Your lack of willingness, your lack of contentment over our betrothal will continue to hold you back." Blinking back her tears, she lifted her chin and regarded him with an almost regal expression, back to being entirely composed once again. "Good evening, my lord."

"Good evening," he replied hopelessly, wishing that he could fade into the shadows and hide there until Miss Weston and the rest of his guests had left his townhouse entirely, leaving him alone with his shame and regret.

CHAPTER EIGHT

*M*arianne did not know what to do with herself. It had been two days since Lord Galsworthy's celebration, two days since he had spoken to her with honesty and truthfulness, and two days since she had felt her heart smash into a million, fragmented pieces.

"Marianne, dear."

Lifting dull eyes towards her sister, Marianne tried to smile but felt entirely unable to do so.

"You cannot still be so broken-hearted, not when you told me you had no affection for the gentleman whatsoever," Harriet murmured, sitting down carefully in a chair adjacent to Marianne. "Whatever occurred that has upset you so?"

Marianne had not spoken a word about Lord Galsworthy's conversation to anyone, not even to Harriet, but Harriet had immediately been able to see that there was a deep sadness growing within Marianne's heart and had surmised that something had occurred between Marianne and Lord Galsworthy.

"You are remembering that Lord Galsworthy and his mother are to dine with us this evening, are you not?" Harriet continued when Marianne said nothing. "Along with a few other guests, of course. You must improve your countenance by then, my dear sister, else everyone shall wonder at your despairing looks and tortured eyes." A small, sympathetic smile crossed her face as she touched Marianne's hand before rising to her feet.

"Let me call for tea," she finished, tugging at the bell pull before seating herself again. "That usually lifts your spirits."

Marianne shook her head. "I do not think that it will do so today, no matter how many cups I drink," she muttered ruefully. "Oh, Harriet, it is all such a tangled mess!"

Harriet frowned. "But why?"

"Because," Marianne said, forcing the words out. "Lord Galsworthy told me he wished for us both to be open and honest with one another, feeling as though we had not done so thus far in our acquaintance and, at his words, I felt my heart lift." She shook her head, angry that she had allowed herself to be so fooled. "We even had a pleasant – nay, an enjoyable – conversation, and he apologized most beautifully for not sending a note the moment he returned to England." From the corner of her eye, she saw Harriet brighten as though such an action spoke of an affection for Marianne but knew that it was not so. "I welcomed it," she continued, looking down at her hands as though it might prevent her from feeling so much pain if she did not look at her sister. "I thought it might allow us to find a degree of happiness, a degree of contentment in our marriage. If we furthered our acquaintance, then there was the possibility that..." Trailing off, she found herself unable to speak any more, her own foolishness screaming at her that she had brought this agony upon herself.

"You thought he might come to care for you," Harriet said softly, evidently seeing what Marianne was trying and failing to hide from her. "You began to feel something for him also?"

"I did," Marianne whispered brokenly. "Oh, Harriet, I am foolish indeed! When we conversed, when he smiled and laughed, I found my heart warming with a fondness for him that had not been there before. His apology only added to it, his genuine wish to be honest and open with me making me feel as though our future could be a happy one. And then, he broke it all apart in a single moment."

Harriet closed her eyes, drawing in a long breath before opening them again as if to steady herself and consider what she was to say. "Is there the possibility that you might have misunderstood him, Marianne?"

"No."

Marianne shook her head blindly, tears blurring her vision. "He stated, quite unequivocally, that he was *resigned* to our marriage." She looked up, tears spilling on to her cheeks. "Resigned, Harriet. It was as though I am a terrible, dark fate that he cannot escape from, that he has finally chosen to accept." Suddenly, the reason for Lord Galsworthy's sudden departure to India became clear.

"He tried to run from it but has discovered he cannot," she whispered hoarsely. "How can I carry on a life with him knowing that, in his heart, that is how he feels about our marriage?"

For a good few minutes, Harriet said nothing. In fact, she sat back in her chair and shook her head, a long slow breath escaping her. Marianne, who had expected her sister to be able to offer some sort of advice, to perhaps even defend Lord Galsworthy, wiped at her cheeks and tried to compose herself. This unburdening of her heart had been cathartic, for she had shared her pain with her sister and now felt the better for it.

"My dear Marianne," Harriet said eventually, reaching across to take her hand for a moment. "I am truly sorry that you were injured so."

Marianne managed a watery smile. "You are not going to defend him?"

"No, not in any way!" Harriet exclaimed, looking a little offended. "What he said to you was both rude and cutting, and I cannot excuse it. No, my dear sister, I can see your pain and I am sorry for it." She tipped her head a little and looked at Marianne carefully. "Is your betrothal at an end, then?"

Marianne shook her head. "No, it is not," she responded bitterly. "I told Lord Galsworthy in no uncertain terms that I expected a proposal very soon. He tried to apologize, you see, tried to state that he had not meant such a thing. Something about how he had once felt about our marriage but attempting to assure me that he did not see it in such a light any longer." Settling her hands in her lap, she looked up at Harriet, her eyes clear of tears. "The proposal, which he has yet to perform, is evidence that he is truly no longer held back by his reluctance to enter into this marriage, although I confess that I do not believe that he no longer feels that way. A gentleman does not run away to India to escape from his betrothed if he is not genuinely reluctant to wed!"

Harriet made to say something but waited until the tea tray was brought. "Mayhap he will surprise you," was all she could say without being able, it seemed, to say anything more encouraging. They drank their tea quietly and soon Harriet reminded her that they would have to prepare for dinner very soon, which Marianne accepted with a good deal of heaviness in her heart. She was tormented by what Lord Galsworthy had said to her, hating that she had allowed her heart to soften towards him, only to be broken down by a single word which had left her utterly devastated.

Foolish, foolish girl for having even the slightest fondness for the gentleman!

"I should go up to change," Harriet said, breaking into her thoughts. "Our guests will be arriving in a few hours and you know how particular Father is."

Marianne nodded and got to her feet, only for the door to open and the butler to step inside, holding a card in his hand.

"My ladies, there is a gentleman who wishes to call upon you both, despite the late hour for afternoon calls."

Marianne took the card and read it, aware of the butler's disapproval of any gentleman who called after visiting hours. Her heart jumped into her throat, only to race back down into her chest, handing the card to Harriet. It was none other than Lord Henry Redmond.

"Where is our father?" she asked as Harriet set the card down. "Is he at home?"

"He is in the study and not to be disturbed for another half hour or so, my lady," the butler intoned. "If you wish it, I can send Lord Henry away with a good excuse, my lady."

Harriet opened her mouth but Marianne immediately spoke ahead of her. "No, you need not do so. Send him in and order a fresh tea tray. We will have a short visit together." She ignored Harriet's warning look, realizing that she had not thought once of Lord Henry these last few days, but finding his company now to be almost a distraction, taking her away from her miserable thoughts of Lord Galsworthy.

"Are you quite sure of this, Marianne?" Harriet whispered as the butler left the room. "What if Father comes in?"

"Then he will think Lord Henry is here on account of you," Marianne replied crisply, praying that she did not look too pale. Pinching her cheeks, she settled herself in her chair again, only to rise gracefully as Lord Henry walked into the room.

"Miss Weston," he said grandly, bowing over Marianne's hand. "And Miss Weston." Having met Harriet on a previous occasion, he greeted her as warmly as he had Marianne before seating himself between them. A tea tray was brought in almost immediately, with their old one taken away by the harassed looking maid. Marianne knew there was a good deal going on below stairs since the dinner was a grand affair with ten guests altogether.

"I do apologize for the lateness of my visit," Lord Henry began, looking at Marianne with a good deal of warmth in his expression. Marianne felt herself smile of her own accord, the first time she had done so in several days, seeing the joy evident in his green eyes at seeing her.

"It is quite all right, Lord Henry," she replied quickly. "We are very glad to see you."

"As am I to see you," he stated, not so much as glancing at Harriet. "I thought to invite you both to my Ball."

"A Ball!" Harriet exclaimed, drawing Lord Henry's attention for the first time. "You are to host a Ball?"

He chuckled. "The grandest you have ever seen, my dear lady. You will both join me, I pray? Your father also, although I understand he is not to be disturbed at the moment, else I would have given him the invitation myself."

A spark of happiness ignited Marianne's heart, her smile spreading all the more. "That sounds quite delightful, Lord Henry," she began, thinking that to dance and converse with gentlemen of the *ton* might help her to forget her increasing unhappiness over Lord Galsworthy. "When precisely is it?"

Lord Henry began to explain, delighting both Marianne and Harriet with the details of all he had planned. Marianne felt her heart lift all the more, her mind no longer caught up with her morose thoughts over Lord Galsworthy. She liked Lord Henry immensely, she had to admit, although she was well aware that she was still very much betrothed to Lord Galsworthy.

Just as Lord Henry rose to his feet, ready to take his leave, the door opened and in stepped none other than Lord Bridgestone, Marianne and Harriet's father. He stopped dead, clearly astonished to see his daughters entertaining a guest when they ought to be preparing themselves for dinner.

"Father," Harriet said quickly, moving towards him. "May I introduce Lord Henry Redmond? Lord Henry, this is our father, Lord Bridgestone."

Lord Henry greeted him with an easy manner. "I believe we have already met at the card table, Lord Bridgestone."

Marianne's stomach tightened, seeing her father study Lord Henry with an almost suspicious air, before, to her utter astonishment, his face broke into a broad smile.

"Yes, of course, Lord Henry! How are you?"

"In excellent health, Lord Bridgestone. I am just come to deliver an invitation to you all to my Ball in a fortnight's time. It would be my very great honour to have you, your wife, and two such fine young ladies attend."

At this compliment, even Harriet smiled and blushed, catching her father's attention. Marianne watched with interest as her father considered Lord Henry for another moment before returning his attention to Harriet. It was obvious that he was considering that Lord Henry, being both titled and wealthy, might be of particular interest to his younger daughter.

"We are to host a dinner this evening, Lord Henry,"

her father said, placing both hands behind his back. "You will join us, of course."

Lord Henry looked surprised. "That is very kind of you, Lord Bridgestone."

"You will be favouring us with your presence," Lord Bridgestone chuckled. "At the moment, our table will seat thirteen guests and we cannot have such a number as that! I believe Lady Galsworthy will go quite into hysterics if she realizes it. No, fourteen will be a most excellent number."

Marianne found herself smiling at this, feeling a good deal of relief that she would have Lord Henry's company even though she would also be faced with Lord Galsworthy's presence. It would be easier to manage, she was quite sure, if Lord Henry continued with his easy manner and delightful conversation.

"Thank you, Lord Bridgestone," Lord Henry exclaimed, turning to Marianne with a wide smile on his face. "I am honoured."

"Lord Galsworthy will join us also, of course," her father continued with a pointed look in Marianne's direction. "You may know some of the other guests but if not, I will be glad to make the introductions." He beckoned to Marianne, who went to his side at once. "Do go and tell the housekeeper to add one more place at the table before you go to change."

Marianne nodded, glancing over her shoulder at Harriet who had come to join her. "Of course, Father," she murmured, catching Lord Henry's eye and seeing him smile at her. Her heart warmed again, chasing away her nervous anxiety over seeing Lord Galsworthy. "Do excuse us, Lord Henry."

He inclined his head. "Not at all, Miss Weston. Miss Weston." He directed his gaze towards Harriet, evidently to satisfy Lord Bridgestone that he had no particular thoughts towards Marianne. Lord Bridgestone appeared pleased with this and suggested that they both have a brandy whilst they waited for the guests and Marianne and Harriet stole from the room.

"Do you think this wise?" Harriet asked, putting one hand on Marianne's arm. "You know full well that Lord Henry is eager to further his acquaintance with *you*, even if he has managed to convince Father otherwise. What if Lord Galsworthy –"

"Lord Galsworthy may watch me converse and laugh with another gentleman for as long as he wishes," Marianne replied stubbornly. "I like Lord Henry, Harriet, although I confess that I feel no particular fondness for him – but he is good company and I am glad to have him join us for dinner."

Harriet let go of her arm and Marianne stalked off ahead, her heart twisting and turning in all directions. She knew to encourage Lord Henry was not exactly wise but the fact that he relieved some of her anxiety when it came to thinking of Lord Galsworthy was all she could consider. She would make sure to look her best this evening and show Lord Galsworthy that he had not injured her in any way, even if the truth was quite the opposite.

CHAPTER NINE

*P*hilip did not much like Lord Henry Redmond.

When the introductions had been made, Philip had recognized Lord Henry at once, although he had not said as much to anyone. Lord Henry was the gentleman whom he had seen taking both Miss Marianne Weston and Miss Harriet Weston out for a carriage ride. Ice had formed in his veins as he'd greeted the fellow, a little confused and also perturbed at the sly smile on the gentleman's face as he'd acknowledged him. It was as though Lord Henry knew that Philip and Miss Weston were betrothed and thought it almost mirthful. The way the gentleman had gone immediately from his side to the arm of Miss Marianne Weston had only increased Philip's dislike of the man. Of course, it had pained him all the more to see Miss Weston laugh and smile in conversation with Lord Henry, hating that he could not garner the same reaction from her himself.

Miss Weston had not come to talk to Philip at all, not

in the hour they had spent talking before dinner. She had greeted him, of course, but there had been no warmth in her smile, no brightness in her eyes. It had been overly formal and painfully tense as they had greeted one another although, for whatever reason, Philip could barely take his eyes from her. Even as Lord Henry had talked to her, even as he'd watched how the man had ingratiated himself with the lady, Philip had been entirely unable to look away.

The emotion he had battled that afternoon in the park had returned to him again. This time, Philip recognized it for what it was, aware that he was both angry and frustrated, but also envious of Lord Henry's seemingly close companionship with Miss Weston. It was all so very strange. He himself had made a terrible mess of things with the lady and yet wanted to draw even closer to her despite it. It was just that he could not find a way to do so. To propose to her, when he was not at all certain that it would bring either of them any happiness, was difficult indeed. Despite this, Philip recognized that his desire for Miss Weston was still there, buried under all of his other confusing emotions. He was always aware of her, always knowing where she was, what she was saying, whom she was talking with. It was as though he could not get enough of her company and yet struggled to find even a single thing to say.

They had been seated at dinner for less than half an hour and, as the time passed, Philip found his dislike of Lord Henry growing steadily. He could not say precisely why that should be, for the man was neither rude nor condescending. In fact, he was jovial and pleasant, enter-

taining the company at large with his humorous remarks
and interesting conversation. Every single person present
seemed more than enamoured of him, even Philip's own
mother. Philip, it seemed, was the only person present
who did not find Lord Henry particularly good company.

His eyes drifted towards Miss Weston, aware that
she was watching Lord Henry with almost rapt attention. Her eyes were bright and there was a light flush in
her cheeks, which only heightened his awareness of her
beauty. He knew full well that he had hurt her terribly
by his foolish and less than considered response to her,
when they had first spoken that night on the terrace, but
he had since found himself quite unable to find anything
to either write or say to her, to bring the matter to a
close. The truth was as he had said it – he *had* been
resigned to their marriage, seeing no way out of it and
quite certain that he would do his duty. However, as
they had talked and laughed together, he had found his
future suddenly appearing a little brighter, his mind
caught with all that might be for him – for them both – if
there was a genuine fondness and friendship between
them. Miss Weston had not been as he had remembered
her. There had been that sharp fierceness which had
quite unnerved him, only for her to soften as he had
apologized. He had been reminded of his jealousy on
seeing her with the gentleman he now knew to be Lord
Henry, realizing that he would not have felt even a
single modicum of emotion had he not any affection or
desire for the lady in question. The way they had slowly
been drawn into what then turned out to be an easy
conversation had brought a lightness to his spirit which

had not been there before, only for him to drag it all back down to the depths with one foolish, thoughtless word.

"I hear you have been in India for the last year and more, Lord Galsworthy."

Philip started in his seat, feeling a flush of embarrassment creep into his face almost at once. He was aware that almost every guest now had their eyes on him whilst he had been lost in thought. Lord Henry was looking at him with a wry smile, evidently aware that he had discomfited him a little, although obviously quite unintentionally.

"Yes, I was," Philip replied in a firm tone of voice that would show, he hoped, that he was not about to be cowed by a little embarrassment. "My father had holdings over there and I thought to go and survey them for myself."

"And it took you a year to do so?" Lord Henry commented, looking shocked. "Goodness, Lord Galsworthy, they must be quite substantial!"

A ripple of laughter went around the table and Philip was forced to lift his chin a notch, a tight smile on his face hiding the twisting of his gut. It was as though Lord Henry wanted to mock him for whatever reason, but he was not about to let himself react to it. "Indeed," he muttered, looking away from Lord Henry and towards Miss Weston, who was steadfastly refusing to so much as glance in his direction. "The passage to India was hard and I confess I tried to delay my return to England for a time, until I was well enough and strong enough to board ship again." It was an outright lie, for he had not been so ill that he could not have returned to England much sooner than he had done, but the truth was not something he was easily able to share.

"My son is most diligent," he heard his mother say, a little surprised at her swift defense of him. "He has always taken the greatest of care when it comes to his responsibilities, particularly when the title came to him." Her smile slipped and a sadness formed in her eyes. "My husband, the late Lord Galsworthy, would have been immensely proud of the man my son has become."

Philip's gaze softened as he caught his mother's eye, finding her to be a good deal more gentle of late. Her words brought him both relief and happiness, glad to know that she did, in fact, think highly of him and that he had not let her down when it came to his responsibilities towards his title and his estate.

"Indeed," Lord Bridgestone said with a meaningful glance towards Miss Weston. "We are very glad to have you join us here this evening, Lord Galsworthy."

"Thank you," Philip replied, his stomach tightening as he saw the dark glance sent his way by Lord Henry, whose smile had faded and whose eyes had narrowed as Lady Galsworthy had begun her kind speech about Philip's attributes. He was relieved when the conversation moved onto something entirely new – the little Season that was soon to begin, and what exciting occasions there might be. He had no thought of the little Season, knowing that he ought to be married by then.

"When do you think to return to your estate?"

Seeing Lord Henry direct him another question, Philip sighed inwardly, aware of how Miss Weston was now, by this point, blushing furiously.

"I have no intention of returning to my estate in the near future," he replied firmly. "I have a few matters to take care of here in London. In fact, I have to consider whether or not I will return at all this year. It may be the start of next year before I decide to reside there again for a prolonged duration."

Miss Weston glanced at him before setting her eyes back down in her lap.

"You will remain in London for the little Season, then?" Lord Henry asked, as the conversation buzzed around them. "You have no urge to go to address your responsibilities at your estate, even after a full year of absence?"

His gut tightened and Philip had to make a concerted effort to hold onto his temper. This gentleman had no knowledge of him at all, and to be making such remarks as these were both rude and entirely inappropriate. "My steward is an excellent man and keeps me informed of all that goes on at my estate," he replied quickly. "Besides, I have a responsibility to take care of my mother and she wishes to remain here for the little Season also."

"I see," Lord Henry murmured, his eyes now flashing with a thinly veiled dislike. "I too hope to remain in town. There are a few acquaintances I wish to further and one cannot do so from one's estate!" He sent a warm glance in Miss Weston's direction and, to Philip's horror, he saw her give the gentleman a tiny smile.

A lump formed in his throat. Lord Henry had managed to elicit something from Miss Weston that he himself had struggled with ever since they had first met, even in the midst of what had been a horribly inelegant discussion. In fact, the first time he had seen her smile at *him* with such freedom had been the evening on the terrace, which he had then gone on to ruin entirely. He watched, helplessly, as Lord Henry quickly managed to strike up a conversation with both Miss Marianne Weston and Miss Harriet Weston, making them both smile and laugh in turn. He was quite forgotten, it seemed. Yet again, there was none of the awkwardness he had so often felt between himself and Miss Weston. In fact, the gentleman had such an ease in his manner that Philip felt quite sure that not a single guest here would be able to turn away from the man, should he catch them in conversation.

Watching Miss Weston, he saw how her lips were curving in an ever ready smile, how her eyes fixed on Lord Henry without any of the uncertain glances that so often had come Philip's way. It was obvious to him that Lord Henry had a fondness for both ladies, although he was well aware of how often Lord Henry addressed Miss Marianne Weston over Miss Harriet Weston. His stomach dropped to the floor and he set down his fork, no longer hungry. In fact, he felt a little nauseous. This was not what he had thought this evening's dinner would be. He had prayed that he would have the opportunity to speak to Miss Weston quietly, to explain to her his foolishness and his awkwardness, to beg her to forgive him – yet again – and to continue their acquaintance with the intention of proposing to her very soon. What he had not ever expected was to see another gentleman capture his betrothed with his smiles and his conversation, drawing Miss Weston away from Philip and towards himself.

*Are you truly going to propose to her, knowing that
you would only make her miserable?*

His pain and jealousy bit at him, hard. If he were to
propose, as she had asked, then he would be tying them
together for the remainder of their days. He would never
be able to bring her such joy as was evidenced here, for,
thus far, he had only made her miserable, hurting her
with his words and turning her away from him entirely. If
he was to propose, then the wedding would take place in
a few short weeks with no opportunity whatsoever for
him to change his mind – or for Miss Weston to change
her mind either. In fact, she had even less opportunity
than him, given that her reputation would be irreversibly
damaged if she thought to break off their engagement
entirely.

What was worse was that he now realized that he
was eager to be as comfortable as Lord Henry was with
the lady. He felt a desperation growing within him, such
as he had never felt before. Part of him wanted to rise
from the table, to push Lord Henry unceremoniously
from his chair, and to take his place, forcing Miss Weston
to speak to him so that they might attempt to find a way
together.

But he knew that would not only be mortifying for
them both, but might, in fact, bring even further difficulties. His heart and mind were going from one place to the
next, clouded with indecision and anxiety. He wanted to
do what was right by Miss Weston and that included
considering her future happiness.

Philip wanted to put his head in his hands right there
at the dinner table, such was the depth of his unwanted

and confusing thoughts. To see Miss Weston so happy in conversation with another gentleman only revealed to him just how poorly he had done thus far. To see her now, smiling and laughing with the same freedom in her expression as he had seen in her at the park when he had first arrived in London tore pieces out of his soul. It was as if he realized too late that Miss Weston was, or could be, a truly wonderful wife, had he only taken the time to talk with her, to further his acquaintance with her. Why had he shied away from it? Yes, he had been afraid and yes, he had not wanted to marry someone his father had simply forced on him, but that was no excuse for his lack of effort. The truth was, he had not needed to run away to India. Had he any courage at all, he would have remained in London and done his duty to Miss Weston as he ought. Perhaps then he would have realized just how blessed he would be to have her as his wife.

Mayhap it was all much too late. He could fall on his knees before her and declare that he had been weak, that he had been a coward, but that he was more determined than ever to prove himself to her. He could tell her of his envy, of his jealousy which had stung him almost incessantly all evening. Would that make her consider him again with fresh eyes? Would she be willing to set aside his past behaviour and see the man he was trying to become?

"Lord Galsworthy?"

Managing to contain his surprise with an effort, Philip turned his attentions back towards Lord Bridgestone, who was looking at him with a broad smile plastered on his face.

"Yes, Lord Bridgestone?" Philip asked, aware that most of the guests had quietened their own conversations in order to listen to their host.

Lord Bridgestone's smile was bright, his eyes glistening as he glanced from Philip to his daughter and back again. A heavy weight settled in Philip's stomach.

"I thought, since you are only just returned to England, that you might wish to say something," Lord Bridgestone replied, as though this was quite the done thing at a gathering such as this. "A toast, perhaps?"

Dread ran all through him, a sheen of sweat appearing immediately on his brow.

"A toast, Lord Bridgestone?" he enquired, feeling quite certain that he knew what Lord Bridgestone expected.

"Indeed," the gentleman replied, gesturing for him to stand. "Speak as freely as you wish, good sir."

Philip rose to his feet feeling a little unsteady, quite unsure as to what to say. It was more than obvious that the gentleman expected him to use this supposedly delightful opportunity to propose publicly to Miss Weston but given what Philip had just seen of her interactions with Lord Henry, he felt entirely unable to do so. In fact, he could not even look at her, hearing the silence fall across the room. Every eye was on him, an air of expectation settling on each and every guest. Philip's mouth went dry and, realizing that he had not picked up his glass, he attempted to do so, almost knocking it over in the process.

A chuckle came from Lord Henry, unsettling Philip further. His face burned with mortification as he cleared his throat, not quite sure where to look. The silence lingered for a little too long, making the guests expectations change into a growing awkwardness that burned into Philip's mind. He could not think what to say, was not even certain that his voice could be trusted to speak whatever words he eventually chose.

"Lift your glasses, everyone."

Philip shot a glance to his mother, who, in her calm, clear voice, had broken the tension and had allowed Philip a moment to himself to gather his thoughts as the guests made sure they each had their glass in their hand, with some requiring their glass to be filled again before they could continue. Philip let out a slow, quiet sigh of relief, finally able to think coherently again. He could not propose to Miss Weston, as Lord Bridgestone expected, not here at this very moment and certainly not when he was no longer certain it would be either right or fair for the lady. Therefore, he would have to think of something else to say, something else with which he could make a toast to.

"Ladies and gentlemen," he began, relieved that his voice was neither weak nor hoarse. "I am recently returned from India, as you all know. I am truly overwhelmed with the welcome I have had since I returned, including this evening's wonderful dinner." He smiled at Lord Bridgestone, who inclined his head but did not smile, seemingly a little puzzled.

"There are several things I still have to consider and a good many decisions which must be made now that I have resumed the responsibilities of the estate and title, but I am quite sure that I will have no difficulty in doing so, not when I have such wonderful friends and family to support such endeavours. Therefore, I would raise a toast to you all, for your warm welcome and your continued friendship. I am glad of it all."

The guests all appeared rather taken with this and smiled, lifted their glasses, and then took a sip, allowing Philip to return to his seat. He could see, from the way that Lord Bridgestone was looking at him, that he was not particularly pleased with the speech and the toast, given that he had evidently expected it to be directed towards Miss Weston. His mother was smiling at him gently, her expression one of understanding. He saw her lean towards Lord Bridgestone and begin to discuss things in low tones whilst the other guests returned to their conversations, and Philip prayed that she would be able to remove any frustration from Lord Bridgestone's mind so that he would not have to deal with the gentleman later. There was too much weighing heavily on his mind for him to have any further conversations which would require any sort of explanation of his lack of willingness to propose outright to Miss Weston.

The rest of the dinner seemed to take an age. Philip said very little to anyone else and was thoroughly relieved when the ladies rose from the table in order to leave the gentlemen to their port. He had no intention of remaining at Lord Bridgestone's house for very much longer. Once the remainder of the evening's events began in earnest – most likely singing, music and mayhap even some dancing – he would remove himself and return home. If anyone asked him, he could simply claim that he was still recovering from his journey home, which he was quite sure everyone would accept without question.

His heart was sore, his mind was clouded. He longed for home, for the silence, broken only by the crackling of the fire. He did not want to be here, not when he knew that he could not make Miss Weston as happy as Lord Henry did. He had realized his need for her too late. He had behaved foolishly, speaking without consideration, and was now bearing the consequences of such behaviour. Whose fault was it other than his own?

The thoughts did not leave him, long after he returned home to his own bedchamber. Even as he lay on his bed, attempting to let sleep take him, his mind would not let go of her. How he longed to see her as she had been that day at the park, with her sparkling eyes and gentle smile! Why could he not bring that joy out in her? Why could Lord Henry so easily manage to do what he could not? And why did the desire to know Miss Weston better refuse to leave him when he already felt as though it was much too late for that?

The vision of her standing before him on the terrace, laughing at a remark he had made, still clung to his mind. That was the lady he wanted, that was the lady he desired to know. No longer did he feel resigned to their marriage, no longer did he feel compelled to turn and run from it. No, he *wanted* to further his acquaintance with her, to consider their future together, turning towards her instead of running from her.

"And it is much too late."

The words echoed through his mind, a cold hand of fear clutching at his heart. He could not let her go, not yet, but neither could he tie her to him forever. The decision would not come, his heart was not settled. It remained torn, agonizingly painful, and Philip finally fell asleep, still in an utter quandary over what he ought to do.

CHAPTER TEN

*M*arianne smoothed her gown with trembling hands, more than a little anxious about what her father would say to her. Having been summoned to his study, she had very little doubt as to his mood, aware that he had been utterly silent last evening on their drive home.

"Come in, Marianne."

Closing her eyes, Marianne swallowed the ache in her throat and, attempting to put a smile on her face, stepped into the study and closed the door behind her.

"Yes, Father?"

To her utter astonishment, he smiled at her, beckoning her over to the two chairs by the fire. When she moved towards him, he took her hands in his and pressed them tenderly, shaking his head as he did so.

"My dear girl," he murmured softly. "How do you fare this morning?"

She did not know what to say, such was her surprise. Her father had never shown such consideration to her emotional state before and, having expected him to be either outwardly furious or white-lipped with inner rage, she felt almost entirely overwhelmed with his consideration of her.

"You are still upset," he continued, pressing her hands. "Do come and sit down, my dear girl."

"Thank you, Father," Marianne managed to say, sitting down carefully, and settling her hands in her lap. "I confess, I thought you would be more than angry with me considering Lord Galsworthy's lack of attention towards me."

He lifted one eyebrow. "I would not be angry with you, Marianne," came the reply. "Why should you think so? It is not anything you have done." His lips tightened, his eyes a little angry as he spoke. "From what Harriet tells me, Lord Galsworthy did not so much as send you a note when he arrived back in London!" Returning his gaze to her, he sent her an inquiring glance. "Is that so?"

Rather thankful that her sister had evidently been talking to their father in her defense, Marianne nodded. "It is, Father."

"I cannot understand it," her father frowned, rubbing his chin as his expression grew confused. "Nothing has changed, for the betrothal still stands. He has not spoken to me about any changes he wishes to make and, therefore, I have no doubt that he intends to wed you. However, even though he was given ample opportunity to propose to you both at his celebration and now at the dinner, he has chosen not to do so! I cannot understand it and I confess, my girl, that I find it a little insulting."

You are not the only one who feels that way, Marianne

wanted to say, but wisely chose to remain silent, given the dark expression on her father's face.

"I think I shall have to say something," her father continued, glancing back at her. "Unless you have already had a private conversation with the gentleman and know something that I do not?"

Marianne shook her head, half wishing that it was so. "I am afraid not, Father."

"Then I will have to speak to the gentleman," he continued, shaking his head. "I have also become aware, Marianne, that Lord Henry appears to be quite taken with you." Seeing her immediate blush, he sighed heavily. "I thought it was to be a match for Harriet, but..." Trailing off, he rose from his chair and wandered to the window, evidently deep in thought. "Lord Henry is not, by any means, an unwelcome gentleman. He is titled, wealthy and would make you an excellent husband. The problem is, my girl, that you are already betrothed."

"I am aware of that, Father," Marianne replied hastily. "I have not encouraged the gentleman, I swear to you."

Her father held up one hand, stemming the flow of words from her lips. "You have been nothing but polite and engaging with everyone, I am well aware of that. Again, you need not fear that I will think badly of you." Tilting his head, he looked at her steadily for a moment, his gaze severe. "Am I that much of a tyrant, Marianne?"

Her breath caught, her fingers twisting together in her lap. "You have never been a tyrant, Father," she managed to say, speaking as honestly as she could. "I have always known that you care deeply about my future."

"And about you," he replied slowly. "When the late Lord Galsworthy approached me about the betrothal, I honestly believed it would be the best situation for you, Marianne, but now, as Lord Galsworthy continues to ignore his responsibilities, I find myself wondering if he is the man that I believed him to be." He reached forward and patted her hand, a small, warm smile on his face. "I have never once considered you to be at fault in this, Marianne. You need not look so fearful."

Her heart slowly resumed a normal pace and Marianne felt as though she wanted to cry, such was the tenderness with which her father was speaking. He sat back in his chair and let his gaze travel towards the fire burning in the grate, doing his best to consider what he ought to do. Marianne remained entirely silent, full of relief that she was not to be thought of as responsible in any way.

"The betrothal has not yet become formally known to all of society," her father murmured slowly, his thoughts evidently settling into a coherent order. "No-one outside Lord Galsworthy's family and this family know of the agreement, although I am sure that some may have begun to consider that a match is soon to be made. Therefore, since it is still quite private, I will allow Lord Henry's presence at our home, so long as Harriet is always in attendance." He looked at her sharply and Marianne nodded quickly. She did not want to do anything that would anger her father and would, of course, ensure that Harriet was always present. The fact that she felt very little for Lord Henry did not matter, for she had to admit that she was more at ease around him than when she was in Lord Galswor-thy's presence.

"Of course, Father," she murmured, dropping her gaze to her hands in deference.

"I will not allow him to attempt to court you or anything of the sort at this present time," her father continued firmly, "But I will allow a friendship to develop between the three of you. As for Lord Galswor-thy..." Shaking his head, Lord Bridgestone grimaced. "I shall consider the matter a little longer before I decide what is to be done."

"That is very wise, Father," Marianne replied quickly. "I thank you for your consideration of me."

That brought a smile to his face, a smile she had not expected. "You are a good girl, my dear child," he said, getting to his feet, and putting one gentle hand on her shoulder. "I would not see you unhappy, not for all the world."

The emotions that ran through her brought fresh tears to her eyes, to the point that she thought she might begin to sob right in front of him. He had never spoken to her with such kindness before, being something of a brusque man, and she was almost overwhelmed by the joy and the relief this brought her. She had always known, always trusted, that her father cared for her in his own way, but to hear him speak to her in such a way now made her heart want to burst from her chest. Blinking rapidly, she thanked him in a low voice and turned to leave the room, wondering why she was constantly being tossed between joy and then pain, struggling to keep herself afloat in a sea of emotion.

"Did you enjoy last evening's dinner, Lord Henry?"

Marianne looked up at the gentleman walking along-side her, seeing him smile back at her. His smile brought no kind of fluttering to her heart, no quickening of her breath as she took him in. She knew now, more than ever, that whilst she considered Lord Henry an almost perfect gentleman, with a kind heart, good conversation, and wonderful manners, there was none of the fondness she had once permitted herself to feel for Lord Galsworthy. It was more than a little frustrating, for she desperately *wanted* to feel such a thing for Lord Henry and, in equal measure, wanted not to feel anything of the sort for Lord Galsworthy!

"I did," Lord Henry replied warmly. "Your father is most kind. He and I had a rather... interesting conversation last evening."

Marianne glanced back at her sister, who was walking only a few steps behind but was clearly attempting to listen to their conversation. Marianne held back for a moment, allowing her to catch up, for fear that Lord Henry would wish to say something a little too personal for her liking, should she remain walking with him alone.

"Indeed?" she asked once Harriet had re-joined them. "I do hope our father did not pry too much, Lord Henry. He is rather firm on some matters and chooses our family's acquaintances very carefully."

"He is very astute to do so," Lord Henry replied with a small laugh. "I feel as though I have passed the test, however, for he told me that I was welcome to call upon you both at any time." His smile, directed to Marianne, told her the true meaning behind his words, and yet she felt no spark of warmth, no lurching of her heart. She was glad of his friendship, yes, but there was not, as yet, anything else between them. Perhaps that did not matter, she told herself, as they continued to walk back towards their father's house. Perhaps it did not matter what one felt for one's spouse, she considered, knowing that if she were to marry Lord Galsworthy, as had been planned, then she would spend her days torn between misery and frustration, hating that she felt any sort of fondness for the gentleman who appeared to care so little for her. Would it not be better to tie oneself to a gentleman who had, in his appearance and his manner, a deep considera-tion for her, even if she felt nothing for him in return? She and Lord Henry, should they continue their acquain-tance, would become friends and nothing more – but surely a friendship was a good foundation for any marriage? Lifting her chin just a little, she smiled back at him and saw the relief jump into his expression.

"I thank you, Lord Henry," she said with a glance towards her sister. "I know that my sister and I are always glad of your company."

Harriet suddenly caught sight of an acquaintance of hers and, begging them to excuse her for a moment, hurried towards the young lady, immediately beginning to talk in excited tones.

"Your sister is very lovely," Lord Henry murmured, his gaze lingering on Harriet for a moment before he returned his attention to Marianne. "I think she will make a wonderful wife to whichever fine gentleman takes notice of her."

A little puzzled by this remark, Marianne nodded. "I am quite sure she will, yes."

"But I cannot be that gentleman," Lord Henry continued, making her stomach twist tightly as he smiled at her. "I have every intention of pursuing you, Miss Weston."

Marianne did not know what to say, her heart in her throat for a long moment. A small trickle of sweat ran down her spine, and she felt entirely flustered as Lord Henry waited for her to speak.

"I have embarrassed you," he said after another minute or two of silence. "I apologize, Miss Weston. I ought not to have been so forward, especially when I am aware that it may be that you are promised to another." She looked up at him sharply and saw him shrug as though she ought to understand *why* he knew of such a thing. "I could not ignore the fact that your father asked Lord Galsworthy to speak last evening, when no-one else was asked thereafter. Nor could I miss the way your father looked at you when Lord Galsworthy spoke, evidently waiting for some announcement or other to be made."

"No announcement has been made, Lord Henry," Marianne interrupted, a little sharply. "But may I commend you on your skills of observation in these matters." He looked quite taken aback, staring at her as though he were quite struck by a new, fresh revelation. "You see, Lord Henry," she continued, feeling embarrassment climb into her cheeks, heating them terribly. "I am not as wonderful as you supposedly think."

The astonished look began to fade and his mouth twitched, laughter entering his eyes. "My dear lady, I may not have felt the sharp edge of your tongue before, but I profess that it does not make me think any the worse of you." She looked up at him then, a little surprised. "I am only glad that your father has agreed to allow me to continue to call upon both you and your sister for the time being," Lord Henry continued, shooting a quick glance in Harriet's direction. "I will not be shy about my intentions, Miss Weston. You know very well that I have thoughts of matrimony."

Marianne shook her head sadly. "You need not waste them on me," she replied firmly. "There are more than a few other young ladies searching for good husbands. Why turn your attention to someone who might never be able to bring you the fulfillment and joy you hope for?"

There passed a long moment between them. Lord Henry took a tiny step closer to her and, whilst not improper, Marianne felt a sudden rush of awareness as he did so. She wanted to step back, to put as much distance between them as she could, but instead she held her ground.

"I confess, Miss Weston, that I cannot get you from my thoughts," he replied softly. "Be you betrothed or free, I cannot stop considering you. The fact that Lord Galsworthy does not seem eager to pursue your marriage gives me hope. For, my dear lady, even if you were to end your betrothal yourself, I would not turn from you, damaged though your reputation may be." Marianne caught her breath at what he had revealed, understanding that he was offering to marry her and save her from any sort of disgrace should she break off her betrothal to Lord Galsworthy. "That being said," Lord Henry continued, choosing his words with a good deal of consideration. "I would not want to push you in either direction, Miss Weston. I do not know how you feel when it comes to your betrothed, and neither do I know what you think of me." A wry smile tugged at his lips, giving his handsome face something of a boyish look. "I understand that we must continue to consider these things in our own way. Therefore, I will leave you for the moment and allow us both to simply continue on as we are for the time being. I am quite sure all will become clear in time."

She nodded numbly, feeling as though her entire being had frozen in place. This was quite overwhelming. She had known that Lord Henry had wanted to further their acquaintance, but to hear that he would marry her should she break off her betrothal to Lord Galsworthy was something else entirely! Somehow, she managed to bid him farewell and, with Harriet now by her side, climbed the stone steps before stepping back into the house.

Harriet was chattering away, but Marianne was unable to give her much of a response. In fact, she begged a headache and went to her bedchamber, where she lay down and closed her eyes, feeling her head heavy with thoughts. There was so much going on within her that she was quite weary of it all and, within a few minutes, sleep had taken her away entirely.

CHAPTER ELEVEN

"Galsworthy? Are you quite ready?"

Philip visibly started, looked down at the letter in his hand, and felt utterly miserable. Managing to call out to his mother that he would be quite ready to go by half past the hour, as they had planned, he sat down again in his study chair and shook his head to himself before placing one hand over his eyes.

He had written to Miss Weston only yesterday, some two days after her father's dinner, apologizing profusely for his lack of thought, his inconsiderate words, and his basic lack of courtesy when it came to consideration of her. There had been so much for him to apologize for and yet, somehow, he had found the words difficult to write. It had taken him near seven attempts before he'd been able to write what he'd felt in his heart. However, on the final attempt, he had chosen to speak as openly as he could, and the words had immediately begun to flow from him. He had told her as much as he could, holding almost nothing back.

Ever since the night of the dinner, he had been thinking of Miss Weston as he had never done before. He had gone over and over what Lord Henry had both said and done, and had considered, then, his own behaviour. Realizing that he had been a fool to go to India and leave her behind had brought about a sudden fierceness of spirit. He would not back down now. He would not allow Lord Henry to march in, headlong, and take Miss Weston from him. Was he not as fine a gentleman as Lord Henry? Yes, he did not have his confidence, his freedom of speaking or the like, but he could still show Miss Weston that he had truly begun to care for her. He could show her his regret over his past behaviour, evidence of his change of heart and prove that he had every intention of caring for her as he ought. All of this he had written to her, going so far as to mention the twinge of jealousy he had felt when seeing her so appreciated by another. He had expressed his heart to her, promising that once they were wed, he would do all he could to prove to her that he was not the unwilling, regretful gentleman she thought him to be. Of course, whether she believed and accepted such admissions from him was quite another thing, however, and it was this that set his heart beating wildly.

Her response to his letter was in his hand. He did not dare open it.

Closing his eyes, Philip could still recall just how much of himself he'd put into the letter he'd written to his betrothed. Try as he might, he still could not find the words to put an end to their betrothal, realizing just how often he had begun to think of her these last few days.

Whenever he closed his eyes, he could see her as she had been on the terrace that night, laughing and smiling in his direction with a happiness he had never seen expressed before. He wanted to see that in her again, he wanted to *be* the gentleman who brought that warm smile to her face. In his heart, Philip knew that he was not willing to let her go, not even if he felt as though she deserved someone better than he.

How he wished he had simply taken the opportunity given him by Lord Bridgestone and proposed to Miss Weston right there at the dinner table, in front of all the guests. Of course, he knew full well that she would have accepted him, given their betrothal, but to the rest of the dinner guests it would have come as a complete surprise – and would have been all around London by the following afternoon had he done so. But no, in his confusion and his foolishness, he had not done as he ought and had missed his opportunity.

Writing to her had, at least, given him the chance to express his regret all over again, praying that it would open up the way for them to begin their courtship once more. He would take her walking or call upon her for afternoon tea once or twice before proposing directly. There would be no more delays, just as long as this letter did not contain her refusal to forgive him.

Steadying himself with a long breath, Philip broke the seal and spread out the letter. Only a few short lines were written within and he ran his eyes over them again and again, feeling it burn into his mind.

'My dear Lord Galsworthy', she had written. 'I accept your apologies and find myself quite overwhelmed with what you have expressed to me. However, I confess that I still cannot be sure whether or not I believe you to be truly devoted to the idea of our marriage. Your actions of late – or lack thereof – do not impress upon me the fervency of your supposed feelings. However, I am glad of your honesty and your willingness to prove as much to me and, as ever, I earnestly await your presence. Yours, etc.'.

It was not a letter that held any particular kind of warmth or affection – not that he could have expected that, of course, given what he had both said and done, but there was a feeling of sadness, of lingering pain and frustration that came through her every word. He could not blame her for being so uncertain of him, his heart a little sorrowful as he read the letter again. They barely knew one another and the behaviour he had demonstrated towards her ever since they had first become betrothed had not been the behaviour of a gentleman willing and earnest to move forward with her towards matrimony.

Neither could he tell, Philip realized, whether or not Miss Weston was stating that she accepted his apology and was now earnestly awaiting his presence simply because she felt she had no other choice. A bride-to-be could not exactly state that she was holding his behaviour against him or that she did not wish to be in his presence – that only came once they were wed, or so it had been suggested! Shaking his head, Philip let out a long, pained sigh, setting down the letter again on the table.

"My lord?"

Looking up, Philip realized that he had not heard the

butler's knock, seeing the man standing framed in the doorway with a rather uncertain look on his face.

"Yes, do come in," he said quickly. "I do apologize if I did not hear you. Is it my mother?"

The butler smiled, taking away some of the gravity from his usual, sombre expression. "No, my lord, it is not," he replied, handing Philip a letter. "Although might I suggest that you present yourself a few minutes before you are due to leave for the theatre? It may help your mother's nerves."

Philip chuckled, breaking the seal at once. "Thank you. I will be sure to do so." Alone once more, he opened the letter and saw that it was from his steward. His gut tightened, reading the lines quickly. What neither his mother nor Miss Weston knew was that he had written to his steward almost as soon as he had returned to England, inquiring about all matters relating to his estate, and querying whether or not he ought to return there at once.

The steward was a hardworking man and had kept on top of Philip's affairs with both dedication and accuracy. However, there was the suggestion near the end of the detailed letter that Philip return to his estate as soon as he could, so that he might make some decisions about matters for which the steward had no authority. Philip felt himself hesitate, knowing that he wanted to return to his estate but also fully aware that he could not leave Miss Weston behind. He had to propose to her – and soon. It would be another month or so before they could both remove to the Galsworthy estate and so, Philip quickly penned a letter in reply to his steward, stating that he would be returning to his estate just as soon as he could, thinking that he would send it in a week or so when matters in London would be a good deal more settled.

That done, and aware that his mother might very well start eating her hat with anxiety, worrying that they would be late for the theatre, Philip made his way out of the study and down the staircase, seeing Lady Galsworthy already waiting for him. Very soon, they were in the carriage and on the way to the theatre with Philip's mind still caught up with his letters.

"Galsworthy?"

"Yes, Mama?"

She tipped her head a little, regarding him. "Galsworthy, might I ask you what is wrong?"

Frowning, he sat back in his seat. "I do not understand what you mean, Mama."

"I mean," she persisted with a sharpness to her voice that reminded him of how severe she could be. "I mean to ask you why you have not yet proposed to Miss Weston. You had the opportunity to do so at Lord Bridgestone's dinner but you did not use it."

His throat tightened but he simply shrugged, trying his best to appear nonchalant. "Mama, I simply did not feel it the most suitable moment. I do not want to propose in public and certainly not when I am pressed to by Lord Bridgestone!"

She frowned but did not immediately respond. Philip prayed that she would accept his excuse, but given the expression on her face, he was quite certain she did not accept one word of it.

"I have done my best to improve my forthright and

often demanding ways of late," his mother said, surprising him with her gentle tone. "I have considered what you said to me, Galsworthy, and have tempered my desire to tell you what to do and when to do it."

He smiled and reached across to press her hand for a moment. "I am aware of that, Mama, and I am grateful for it."

A smile crossed her face, softening her eyes. "Thank you, Galsworthy. However, in this matter, I cannot believe that you wish to propose to Miss Weston alone, not when you have not so much as called on her again since that evening."

Closing his eyes, Philip let out a breath. "Mama, pray, do not press me."

"I only want to be of assistance to you, Galsworthy!" she exclaimed, sounding rather hurt at his request that she stop her questioning. "Who have you to talk to? Who have you to share with? Who is there to advise you in this matter, other than your own self?"

Philip wanted to keep everything within, telling himself that he did not need his mother's counsel, only to hear himself begin to speak. His words tumbled from his mouth as he told his mother almost everything that had been on his mind of late. To his surprise, she did not appear astonished or upset, but rather nodded slowly, as if she had been expecting this.

"My dear boy," she said when he had finally finished speaking. "What a tangle you have made." Her expression was one of sympathy but Philip could barely acknowledge it, feeling as though he had let himself drain away entirely, given all of his strength and effort into such a simple thing as sharing what was on his mind.

"You must be honest with her, as you have said you will be," his mother continued as the carriage began to slow. "Tell her all that you have told me."

Philip recoiled from the idea at once. "Mama, I could not!" The thought of confessing to Miss Weston that he regretted his lack of consideration for her, that he felt utterly foolish at having spoken without careful thought, that he now began to feel something for her that had taken him completely by surprise, sent icy water trickling down his spine. "Besides which, I have already written to her to confess... most of what I have told you."

His mother shook her head. "*Most* is not *all*, Galsworthy. You have not, I surmise, told her your sudden affection for her, your sudden desire to be in her company as often as you can manage it." She lifted an eyebrow and Philip was forced to look away, knowing that she spoke the truth. "You have not confessed to her your fears that you are much too late, that you might never convince her of your change of heart. Be truthful and honest with her, Galsworthy, in everything. Only then can you find the happiness you are so desperate to have."

Philip tried to nod but found himself frozen in place, the idea of sharing his very heart with his bride to be making him almost nauseous. Of course, he did want to develop that intimacy which came with being husband and wife, but surely that took time? He could not imagine saying the words, 'I have been so afraid that I might lose you to another' to her, his heart quickening with fright at the very thought. Given that he could barely find the words to write a coherent letter to her, he did not think that he would manage to speak to her so.

"You must call on her soon," his mother warned as the carriage came to a stop in front of the theatre. "And if you are to evidence your intentions, as you have stated, then you must propose to her almost immediately," she continued, patting his hand as the carriage door swung open. "She is a lovely young lady and I know you will be happy together. You simply have to sort out this tangle first."

Philip nodded. "I will do, Mama," he agreed, finding that, were he honest with himself, he had very little hope that he would be successful in doing so.

CHAPTER TWELVE

"Goodness!"

Philip looked up sharply as his mother made her exclamation, having been busy studying the crowd beneath his box. The theatre was always rather busy and there were many society folk about. It was the place to see and to be seen, and very often it appeared as though the ladies of the *ton* spent most of the performance spying on others through their opera glasses, rather than looking towards the stage! He found no particular joy in studying the *ton*, but one could not help the occasional once-over.

His mother caught his elbow, her fingers tight. "Galsworthy, your betrothed is sitting with another gentleman! A gentleman that is not her father."

Philip swallowed hard, his entire body suddenly swirling with dread. "Oh?"

"Wait a moment."

To his embarrassment, his mother pulled out her

opera glasses and immediately trained them on the box to his left, making him cringe with shame.

"It is Lord Henry Redmond!" she stated in a loud, indignant whisper. "Oh, look! They have seen me." Setting down her opera glasses, she waved over Philip's shoulder, forcing him to turn his head so that he might incline it in greeting.

Miss Weston was seated at the edge of the box, closest to his own. He could make out her expression clearly, seeing the lack of welcome on her face. There was not so much as a smile but instead a rather tight expression that spoke of tension and fright. Obviously, she had not expected to see him in attendance this evening.

"We must go to speak to them during the intermission," Lady Galsworthy said matter of factly. "This simply will not do."

"Mama," Philip replied, hesitating for a moment. "I do not think that we need to..."

"You leave everything to me," his mother replied firmly, interrupting him. "I will make sure that you and Miss Weston are seated together for the second half of the performance, and that Lord Henry is nowhere to be seen."

Philip wanted to argue, wanted to tell his mother that she need not do so, but he held himself back. If he wanted to marry Miss Weston, if he wanted to prove that he was no longer disinclined towards matrimony, then he had to take every opportunity that came his way. He would not propose to her tonight, for it was much too soon after their recent difficulties for that, but he would ask if he could call on her tomorrow, he decided. Yes, that would be the thing. If he could leave the theatre knowing that their courtship was to resume the following day, then he would be pleased with that.

All through the first half of the play – which was, from what Philip saw, a somewhat less than exciting version of 'Romeo and Juliet' – he felt himself growing increasingly aware of his bride-to-be and her presence within the theatre. He found his eyes searching for her in the gloom, glancing towards Lord Henry's box almost every minute as though desperate for her to return his gaze. The intermission came quickly enough and Philip felt his heart quicken as his mother sent a footman to bring both Miss Harriet Weston and Miss Marianne Weston to their box, dispatching another to fetch some champagne. He held himself stiffly, his heart thundering wildly in his chest as he waited for them to arrive.

"Ah, Miss Weston!" His mother rose from her chair almost at once, greeting Miss Harriet Weston whilst Miss Marianne Weston stepped hesitantly towards him.

Goodness, he had never seen anyone so beautiful.

Her hair was held back in a most ornate fashion with only a few wisps escaping around her temples. Her eyes, dark in the shadowy light of the theatre, looked from here to there, never settling on anything for long. More than aware that she was terribly anxious, he stepped forward and took her gloved hand in his.

Her eyes shot to his at once and he held her gaze steadily, almost feeling her tension thrumming through her. "Miss Weston," he murmured before pressing his lips to her gloved hand. Hearing her catch her breath filled him immediately with a deep, cleansing warmth that sent a smile to his lips which, after a moment, Miss Weston returned, albeit with a good deal of uncertainty.

"Thank you for your letter, Miss Weston," he managed to say, his eyes catching a glimpse of Lord Henry coming into the box. "It has done me the world of good to read it. I confess that I have been utterly foolish, as you well know. I truly am sorry for the pain my idiocy has caused you."

She took her hand from his and clasped them together in front of her. "You need not apologize again, Lord Galsworthy," she replied without any particular tone in her voice. "Your letter already sufficed."

He did not know what to say to this, seeing how she looked over her shoulder towards her sister and Lord Henry, whom Philip was forced to greet. Thankfully, he also had to greet Miss Harriet Weston, which brought him a little relief. Soon, they all had a glass of refreshing champagne in their hand and were each sitting comfortably – if not a little cramped – in Philip's box.

"And how do you fare, Lord Henry?" Lady Galsworthy asked with a hint of ice to her words. "Are you to be in London for long?"

The gentleman did not appear put out by the frosty tone and grinned contentedly. "Indeed, I intend to remain in London until the little Season is completed," he replied with a shrug. "In fact, I am considering purchasing property in Grosvenor Square."

Philip raised his eyebrows, seeing his astonishment reflected in his mother's expression. "Do you not already have a townhouse?"

"Yes," Lord Henry agreed slowly, as though deep in thought. "But I confess that it is not adequate for my needs, or should I say that it will *not* be adequate for my needs in due course." On saying this, he shot a glance towards Miss Marianne Weston who looked away immediately, her head lowering just a little, although Philip caught sight of her red cheeks before she could hide them. Anger burst all through him. Lord Henry was making his intentions towards Miss Marianne Weston quite apparent and he simply could not stand for it. The urge to propose to Miss Weston grew steadily and for a moment, Philip considered doing so almost at that very moment, even if only to wipe the simpering, self-satisfied smile from Lord Henry's face.

Lady Galsworthy was the first to speak. "I see," she murmured thoughtfully. "I quite understand, Lord Henry." Clearing her throat a little, she turned towards Miss Marianne and Miss Harriet with a bright smile on her face. "Now, Miss Weston, Miss Weston – might I beg a favour from you?"

The ladies looked a little surprised but nodded.

"But of course," Miss Marianne Weston said, leaning forward a little in her chair. "What is it, Lady Galsworthy?"

"Oh, it is something you will find quite ridiculous, I am sure," Lady Galsworthy continued, "And it will put you both quite out of sorts, I am afraid, but this box is, I find, rather draughty." She put a sad smile on her face and gestured down to her toes hidden beneath her voluminous skirts. "Being of an advanced age, I find myself growing rather cold to the point that I am simply unable to concentrate on the performance. Might I beg of you to sit with Lord Henry in his box?" She did not so much as glance at Lord Henry, as if she did not need his permission and, just as Philip had expected, the two ladies agreed at once. It gave him a sense of satisfaction to see Lord Henry's disgruntled expression, particularly when Lady Galsworthy rose to her feet and asked him to accompany her back to his own box, informing Lord Henry that she wanted to hear all about the property he was considering.

Philip felt his shoulders slump with relief, his tension draining away as Lord Henry was taken away by Philip's mother, leaving him alone with Miss Marianne Weston and Miss Harriet Weston. There was not long left of the intermission at this point and so, thinking that they had best decide which seats to take, Philip put the comforts of the box to the ladies' disposal.

Miss Harriet Weston flashed him a quick look just as the announcement was made that the second half of the performance was about to begin. "I find that I much prefer to sit here at the back of the box," she said with an innocent smile, walking towards one of the seats. "I confess my weakness is to spy on those who have also come to the theatre this evening, and so I have not paid much attention to the performance itself."

"Nor have I," Philip replied with a chuckle. "Are you quite sure, Miss Weston? That is rather far away and I –"

"Do not worry on my account," Miss Harriet Weston replied, sitting down at once and pulling out her opera glasses. "Although I would beg of you both to sit at the other side of the box so that I might have a clear view of the *ton!*"

Miss Marianne Weston laughed at this, shaking her head at her sister and Philip found himself joining in. Their eyes met and Miss Marianne's smile remained on her lips as they sat down together, she seemingly quite willing to be by his side.

"I have done you a great wrong, Miss Weston, and I cannot thank you enough for your willingness to give me another opportunity to prove myself," Philip began as he sat down opposite her. "I know you stated that my letter was more than enough but I cannot help but feel that I must prove myself to you."

"And so you must," she replied without hesitating. "I will not pretend that I have not been quite miserable about the whole thing of late, Lord Galsworthy."

He was a little taken aback by her honesty but found himself nodding in agreement, knowing that he was the cause of such a thing.

"Might I ask you a direct question, Lord Galsworthy?"

"Of course," he murmured, seeing the actors return to the stage. "You may ask me anything you wish, Miss Weston. I am at your disposal."

She did not smile, although her eyes searched his face. Philip felt his heart quicken, his stomach flooding with nerves as he waited, suddenly desperate to reach forward and take her hand in his.

"Why do you wish to marry me?"

The question threw him completely. Staring at her, he felt himself sink into his chair, a wave of freezing water pouring over him as he struggled to find an answer. His limbs were frozen in place, his mouth refusing to move. Even his mind refusing to think of anything coherent.

"Is it simply because we are betrothed?" she asked when he said nothing. "Is that what this is to you, Lord Galsworthy? An agreement that must be honoured?"

"I – I believe that honour is of great value," he stammered, now feeling heat rising up into his cheeks, forcing his tongue to move. "My word has been given and I will honour it."

This answer seemed to disappoint her. The light in her eyes began to fade and she seemed to sink into herself. "I see," she replied softly, looking out towards the stage.

Tell her what is in your heart.

His mother's words came back to him but Philip could not think of how to begin. He ran over a few sentences in his mind, wincing inwardly at how crass they sounded.

"I – I enjoy your company, Miss Weston," he eventually managed to say, knowing that this was only the beginning of all that was in his heart.

She turned back to him, her face expressionless. "Is that so, Lord Galsworthy?"

"Yes," he promised with as much fervour as he could manage. "Yes, it is."

"And when did you start to enjoy my company?" she asked, arching one eyebrow. "Was it before or after you left for India?"

His heart dropped. "That was before I realized just

how I felt," he said, suddenly desperate to make her understand. "That was foolish of me, Miss Weston, and I will own it entirely. I wanted to run away from my responsibilities because I was afraid. This betrothal was thrust upon me without any prior knowledge of it and I –"

"You were not the only one afraid," she interrupted as the actor on the stage began a passionate speech that seemed to entwine itself with Miss Weston's impassioned words. "You were not the only one taken completely by surprise by this news, Lord Galsworthy. However, you were the only one able to make such an escape, whilst I remained here in England, not knowing when you were to return."

Pressing his lips together for a moment, Philip felt the old, familiar guilt begin to creep up on him again. "I am aware of that, Miss Weston," he admitted quietly. "I ought not to have gone to India. I see that now." On impulse, he reached for her hand and took it in his, aware of how she visibly startled at the contact. Holding it tightly, he felt a flood of warmth race up his arm, seeing her looking down at their joined hands before slowly raising her eyes to his.

"Your letters mean more to me now than they did then," he promised, seeing her eyes widen slightly. "I read them often, Miss Weston. They reminded me of home and what I had left behind. I believed myself still reluctant but since I have returned home, an entirely different emotion has filled me. To know that you were, as you said, 'earnestly awaiting my return', made me think often about my estate, my family, and my responsibilities.

Without them, then I might still be in India, hiding from my duties... and from this. Through your letters, I discovered what I had truly left behind." On saying this, he sent a pointed look down towards their joined hands, feeling his heart beating faster as he did so. He had laid out as much of his heart as he could, not quite admitting that he felt more for her than he had ever expected but telling her as much of his truth as he could manage. She did not pull her hand away from his but rather continued to look back at him steadily, her eyes fixed on his as though searching for the truth in his gaze.

"That pleases you, I hope, to hear this," he stammered when she said nothing. "I am not pretending to feel such things as I have stated, Miss Weston – Marianne."

At this, she pulled her hand away slowly, settling them both in her lap. "Miss Weston, if you please, Lord Galsworthy."

He frowned. "My dear lady, if we are to be wed, then surely we can allow ourselves a little intimacy."

"Once you have proposed to me, then perhaps," she agreed with a slight lift of her shoulders. "But as that has not yet occurred, I am of the mind that we should remain in all propriety."

The desire to fall on his knees and ask her to wed him battled at Philip's heart for a moment, but he pushed it aside. There was still pain, still mistrust on her part, and he wanted to remove such emotions from her before he did so. That would require him to court her, as he had planned.

"Then might I call on you tomorrow afternoon?" he

asked slowly. "I have been neglectful of you and I do not wish to be so any longer. I hope to resume our courtship, Miss Weston, if you will allow it."

A tiny smile caught her lips but it was gone in a moment. "Tomorrow afternoon would be more than suitable, my lord."

He inclined his head, feeling a sense of relief fill him. "Thank you, Miss Weston. I am looking forward to it already."

Turning her gaze back towards the theatre stage, Miss Weston let out a long, audible sigh. Philip wanted to ask her what the matter was, wanted to reach for her again, but forced himself to remain where he was. He could not push her, not yet. Not when she was still so vulnerable, still so unsure of him.

"This play always has such a tragic ending," she murmured as he settled his gaze on the stage, just as she did. "There is always so much death, so much pain, so much to endure." Glancing at him, her lips tugged into a rueful smile. "And all because of a misapprehension, is it not?"

Philip considered this for a moment, wondering what Miss Weston was trying to say by such a statement. "And yet, I find myself almost jealous of the two characters in this play, Miss Weston. They had such a love for one another that nothing could break it apart. Only death took one from the other and, even in that, they were joined in the end. To find such a love, such a passion as that must be very rare indeed, I should imagine."

She blinked, her color rising just a little, as though

she had not expected him to make such a considered remark.

"You think about such things as that?" she asked a little cautiously. "You think of love?"

"Is that not what every person thinks of?" he asked, feeling his heart opening towards her all the more. "Is that not everyone's desire? To be able to love freely and to know that one is loved in return, just as our fated Romeo and Juliet did?" They shared a glance and Philip felt his heart lift in a sudden delight. There was something between them now, he could feel it. Something that he prayed would only grow and flourish so that they might step forward into matrimony and happiness.

The rest of the evening was spent talking about all manner of things, with neither Miss Weston nor Philip paying any particular attention to the play itself. They bid each other goodnight and, as Philip pressed his lips to Miss Weston's hand, he saw her blush and look away. That gave him more joy that he could express and he found himself smiling all the way home.

CHAPTER THIRTEEN

"You appear to be in rather better spirits these days, my dear."

Marianne looked up from the letter she was writing to find her father looking at her with a fondness she had not expected to see. "Thank you, Father," she said, putting down her quill. "I feel a good deal better."

Her father nodded sagely, as though he knew precisely why such a thing was. "Indeed. You have Lord Henry to thank for that, I think."

"No, Father, I –"

Waving a hand, her father came over to her and pressed her shoulder lightly, dropping a kiss to the top of her head. "I am just glad to see you so changed, my dear."

"Thank you," Marianne whispered, tears beginning to flood her eyes almost at once, such was the kindness of her father. Ever since their conversation almost a week ago, he had changed in his manner towards her substantially. It was as though he realized that he had not been as considerate as he had thought and she could not help but appreciate that.

"Now, about Lord Galsworthy," he continued, coming around to face her. "I have considered the matter at length."

Marianne's stomach began to swirl. "He has been very attentive these last few days," she interrupted, conscious that her father might not be aware of this fact, given that he had been in his study or out of the house whenever Lord Galsworthy had come to call. "Do you remember I spoke you last evening of the walk we had taken in the park only yesterday?"

Her father frowned. "Yes, I am more than aware of that, Marianne, but one thing still concerns me." Looking at her steadily, he spread his hands. "He has not yet proposed to you."

"That is because we are courting," Marianne explained, unwilling to admit that she found herself still a little confused over her betrothed. "He is ensuring that we know one another well enough before the banns are called."

Lord Bridgestone did not look particularly convinced. "I had intended to speak to him directly," he murmured, frowning hard. "I think it best to remind him of his betrothal and his responsibilities to you. Indeed, I had not thought of staying in London for the little Season also, for I had thought you would be married by then, and Harriet can find herself a gentleman next Season, but now it appears as though we are to linger in London longer than I had planned. I confess, I do not like to linger, not when there appears to be no purpose to it."

His frown lifted slightly as he turned considering eyes onto her. "But, then again, there is still Lord Henry. He is still eager to court you but, of course, I have not given him permission. Perhaps I ought to inform Lord Galsworthy of this so that he might either propose to you or allow you to be free from the betrothal."

"Father, please," Marianne interrupted hastily. "You need not say a word to Lord Galsworthy. Our acquaintance is improving with every day that passes and I do not wish anything to occur that might bring any sort of difficulty to what has already been a trying situation."

This did not appear to please her father, for he muttered something gruffly under his breath, shaking his head to himself before sighing heavily. "Very well," he said after a few moments. "But if nothing has occurred before this time next week, then I shall speak to Lord Galsworthy myself, Marianne."

"Thank you, Father," Marianne replied, her stomach swirling with tension. "I quite understand."

He left the room still murmuring darkly, leaving Marianne to sit back in her chair awash with a sudden relief. Closing her eyes, she drew in her breath slowly, forcing her heart to settle back into its usual rhythm. Everything she had said to her father was quite true, for she did not wish him to speak to Lord Galsworthy simply because they had been rubbing along rather well together the last few days. He had done as he had promised, calling upon her every afternoon and taking her either for a walk about the park if it was not too cold, or to the book-shop, always accompanied by Hetty, for propriety's sake. Marianne found that she was rather looking forward to his company now, feeling a swell of excitement catch at her as she glanced at the clock, knowing it was but a few hours until she saw him again.

Returning to her letter, she continued writing quickly, even though it was only a few lines she intended to write. Reading it over, she found herself smiling happily as she finished it with the words, 'Earnestly awaiting your return', before signing her name.

For whatever reason, over the last week, she and Lord Galsworthy had begun to exchange letters. She had been most surprised when the first one had arrived at her door the morning after their visit to the theatre, breaking it open to read the words written within. It had been very short but had thanked her for her company the previous evening and told her just how much he was anticipating his visit to her that same afternoon. She had not written back to him until the evening, once he had left from his afternoon call. She mentioned how glad she had been of his conversation and his company, hesitating only once before finishing her letter with the words she had always used.

Even now she wrote them, discovering that in her heart she truly was looking forward to being in his company once more.

Sanding it, she quickly folded it up, sealed it and rang the bell, waiting for the maid before telling her to send the letter to Lord Galsworthy at once. Then, with only an hour or so before he was due to arrive, she hastened up to her room to prepare herself for his visit.

As the maid restyled her hair, Marianne reflected on just how much things had changed in her own heart with regard to Lord Galsworthy. This time last week, she had been utterly broken-hearted, convinced that Lord Galsworthy would never feel anything real for her and that he would go into their marriage with reluctance and unwillingness. Now, she felt herself convinced that this was not the case, that her betrothed was, in fact, almost eager to wed her. The way he had spoken deeply, so honestly, about the love that he believed almost everyone longed for had spoken to her heart. She had seen the vulnerability deep within him and had responded to it. Had he not been honest with her, then she might never have known that he too longed for the same things as she: to have love dwelling in her heart, and to have that love returned. Of course, having had an arranged betrothal, she had never considered that such a thing would be possible, but mayhap, in time, it might blossom between them. There was certainly an affection for him now in her own heart and she was quite sure he felt something akin to her own affection, for the way he looked at her now was so very different. There was a warmth in his gaze, a happiness in his smile that had not been present before. It was as if, having moved past the difficulties which had first met them, they had begun to uncover one another's true self. Marianne found herself more free in his company than she had ever been before, although why he had not yet proposed to her, she could not say. That was the only difficulty which still lingered in her mind, still tore at her heart. Was there a reluctance there? Or was it that he simply desired to know her better before the banns were called?

"Mayhap I should ask him," she murmured to herself,

startling the maid who was just finishing with her hair. Flushing, Marianne waved for her to finish before deciding to keep the rest of her thoughts entirely to herself.

"May I say that you look quite wonderful this afternoon, Miss Weston?"

A blush caught her cheeks. "Thank you, Lord Galsworthy," she replied as the carriage came to a stop. "You are very kind."

He smiled at her, his eyes brightening with warmth. "It seems we have arrived," he stated as the carriage door opened.

Marianne did not hesitate, climbing out carefully. Hetty followed them, closely, but not so closely as to intrude upon their privacy. Lord Galsworthy offered her his arm and she took it at once, feeling her heart swell within her as she did so.

"Now," Lord Galsworthy said, spreading his arm out towards the magnificent building before them. "This gallery ought to delight and entertain you quite thoroughly, Miss Weston. And, if it does not, then I must pray that my conversation does so instead. Given my previous failures, I can only hope that it will do so today."

She laughed and patted his arm as they began to walk together, eliciting a wide grin from him. "You need not think so poorly of yourself any longer, Lord Galsworthy. Your conversation has much improved this last while. In fact, I greatly enjoy conversing with you."

His smile faded but was replaced with a look of delight. "Is that quite so, Miss Weston?" he asked, looking at her with such an intensity that it quite took her breath away. It was as if he was not quite sure whether or not he could believe her.

"It is quite true, I assure you," she stated firmly, seeing his expression of sheer joy, which brought a smile to her own face. "I think we are rubbing along quite well together, Lord Galsworthy."

"You cannot know how much joy that brings me," he replied in a voice which was a little tight with emotion. "I have always feared that I..." He trailed off, not looking at her as his jaw worked for a moment. They had stopped walking by now and her hand slid from his arm as she turned to face him, wanting to look into his face.

Lord Galsworthy still remained silent. She waited, her heart quickening all the more. "What did you fear, Lord Galsworthy?" she asked, unable to bear the silence as he still let his gaze drift away from her.

"I have always feared that I was making you deeply unhappy by insisting we honour our betrothal," he said slowly. "I was torn over it for some time, I will admit, but I simply could not let you go, even if I saw that you could have found happiness with another."

Slowly, his gaze lifted and Marianne felt herself shiver with the intensity of his eyes. She trembled violently as he took her hand, looking deeply into her eyes.

"Have I chosen the wrong path?" he asked, his voice a little hoarse. "Did I take you from the better, more deserving gentleman?"

In a rush, Marianne realized that Lord Galsworthy was talking of none other than Lord Henry, and a flush crept into her cheeks almost at once. "My lord, Lord Henry is nothing more than an acquaintance. Whilst I will admit he has been more than attentive; my heart has never pined for him. You need not concern yourself with that." Although, Marianne had to admit that to know that Lord Galsworthy had been considering her so carefully, had been willing to give up their betrothal so that she might be happy and content, meant a very great deal to her. That was kindness itself, that was the consideration and the care she had always hoped to see. Her heart swelled with a sudden, strong affection and she squeezed his hand. "You need have no doubts about my contentedness in this situation, my lord," she finished reassuring him. "I am more than happy, I assure you."

The smile on his face was one of relief and, turning, he offered her his arm, which she accepted without hesitation.

"Come, Miss Weston," he began, clearly delighted with what she had shared with him. "Let me endeavour to make you as happy as you have made me this afternoon." So saying, he led her into the gallery and their afternoon together began.

"You look very contemplative, Miss Weston."

Marianne started visibly, only to feel Lord Galsworthy's hand on her arm for a moment as though to steady her. Heat pooled in her belly, sending sparks all through her as she turned a little to look at him.

"Are you quite all right, Miss Weston?"

"This caught my attention," she murmured, gesturing

towards the large painting that hung on the wall of the gallery. "It seems so... freeing."

Lord Galsworthy turned to study the picture himself, his expression growing dark for a moment. Marianne wondered at it, for the painting was one of the sea crashing wildly onto the shore. There was such beauty in the strokes that she felt as though she herself were almost standing in the middle of the beach, letting a handful of sand run through her fingers, the chill sea air blowing through her curls.

"The sea is not a place I consider favourable," Lord Galsworthy murmured, shaking his head to himself before turning to face her. "The voyage to India was not one that I enjoyed in any way, although it was a little easier on the return."

She turned to him, having quite forgotten that he had sailed so far across the world. "Oh, but did you never once feel the sense of freedom this picture conveys?" she asked almost breathlessly. "Did you never once stand on the deck and stare out at the wide expanse in front of you, without having any idea as to where you were?" She sighed dramatically, one hand pressed to her heart. "I would give anything to see the ocean."

He lifted an eyebrow. "You have never seen the ocean?"

"Never," she replied emphatically. "I do hope to see it one day soon, although I cannot say when." She smiled softly, feeling her heart quicken with nervous anticipation as she continued to speak. "Mayhap my wedding trip might be the opportunity I have been waiting for."

Lord Galsworthy seemed to jerk a little at this but,

much to her relief, he smiled and did not appear to be in any way ill at ease as she had expected.

"Perhaps it would," he agreed, offering her his arm again. "Might you like to walk a little further through the gallery with me, Miss Weston? There are, I am quite sure, several more paintings to see."

"But of course."

As they walked into a smaller, rather dark room, which appeared to be filled with a good number of sombre paintings, Marianne became all the more aware that her heart had not slowed down its frantic pace in any way whatsoever. In fact, it had quickened all the more as she had taken his arm and now the urge to stay close to him continued to grow. The room was entirely empty, other than a gentleman seated in the corner who, she presumed, was meant to ensure that no-one touched nor took any of the paintings. However, it appeared as though he was sound asleep and he certainly did not even move as they walked into the room.

"This is a little melancholy," Lord Galsworthy murmured quietly, drawing closer to a few paintings on the wall. "I would never have any such works in my home, for I fear they are much too gloomy."

She laughed and pressed his arm. "On this matter, I quite agree, Lord Galsworthy. I prefer paintings which are brighter and more cheerful, and intend to fill my home with all such manner of things which will make me smile every time I see them."

He turned to her then, letting her hand free of his arm. "*You* make me smile almost every moment that I am with you, Miss Weston," Lord Galsworthy said, his voice quiet but his eyes filled with a deep intensity that sent a trembling all through her. "I have never deserved to have been given a second chance to prove myself, but your kind heart and sweet nature have blessed me with more than I have ever deserved." His jaw worked for a moment but he did not remove his gaze from hers. "I ought never to have turned my back on you and run, Miss Weston."

Her heart softened. "You need not apologize again, Lord Galsworthy. You have done that so many times that I fear you believe I hold a grudge against you when the opposite is true."

He lifted an eyebrow. "The opposite?" he asked softly.

Butterflies filled her stomach. "Indeed," she admitted, forcing herself to be truthful with him, just as he had promised to be with her. "I feel my heart is opening towards you, Lord Galsworthy. I confess that I was never certain about our betrothal but over this last week, I have found myself almost looking forward to the event."

Pressing his lips together, Lord Galsworthy closed his eyes for a moment before opening them again. "My dear Miss Weston," he breathed as though he could not quite take in what she had said. "There is something I must ask you."

Every part of her stiffened at once, a tension running through her that quickly changed to excitement. She knew what he wanted to ask her, knew that he was about to ask her to become his wife and certainly knew what her answer would be. There was no doubt in her mind now, no fear that she would be married to a man who either regretted marrying her or hated every moment of his married life due to being forced into the situation. Lord Galsworthy had proven himself to be dedicated and more than willing to proceed and for that, as well as for the state of her own heart, Marianne knew she could not refuse him.

Lord Galsworthy let out a long breath, stepping a little closer with one arm now sliding about her waist. Marianne closed her eyes, drawing in a shaky breath, only to feel his breath whispering across her cheek. Just as she opened her eyes, she felt his lips touch her own and jumped violently. Lord Galsworthy stammered and stepped back immediately, leaving Marianne in a state of utter confusion.

"You – you need not apologize, Lord Galsworthy," she managed to say, feeling as though the moment had passed from them entirely. "I simply was not quite prepared." She smiled at him, aware that there was a sudden, desperate longing to have him kiss her again. "Please," she continued, her voice lower and softer. "Do as you were going to, Lord Galsworthy."

Lord Galsworthy drew in a long breath and made to step forward just as four other visitors walked into the room, murmuring to one another in quiet voices. They ignored Lord Galsworthy and Marianne entirely but, with their presence in the room, whatever Lord Galsworthy had been about to say or to do was now entirely impossible.

"Another time, I hope," Lord Galsworthy murmured, taking her hand again. "Forgive me for being so forward, Miss Weston."

"You may call me 'Marianne', if you wish it," Marianne replied, wishing to goodness that those other guests had not interrupted them in the way they had done, else she might now be kissing Lord Galsworthy! "I think it is quite proper for such a thing to occur now."

Lord Galsworthy chuckled. "I am inclined to agree with you, Miss Weston. Very well. Marianne, it is." He looked down at her and smiled and she was relieved to see a slight flush to his cheeks, which matched her own. "We shall continue our conversation at another time, I think. When we are less likely to be interrupted. What say you to that?"

"I should like that very much," Marianne replied, feeling anticipation rising in her chest as they walked together. Suddenly everything seemed brighter, her future happy and settled. All Lord Galsworthy had to do now was propose.

CHAPTER FOURTEEN

The following afternoon, having been reminded that there were now only three days until Lord Henry's Ball, Marianne and Harriet had gone into town in order to purchase one or two new ribbons which they might add to their dresses for the evening. Harriet appeared to be in good spirits, which she claimed was entirely due to Marianne's growing contentedness with Lord Galsworthy. She stated quite firmly that since Marianne was now no longer distraught and upset, it made her feel all the more at ease with the entire situation, glad to know that her sister would be married and settled very soon.

"Of course," Harriet continued as they climbed the steps to the front door of the house, "most of all, I am happy that you are content with Lord Galsworthy. After all you have endured, after all you have gone through with him, I am glad that you have decided upon him once and for all."

"I have," Marianne replied, sighing just a little as she

did so. "He is a good man, I think. He has made some mistakes, but he has owned them and begged my forgiveness on so many occasions that I find myself growing quite weary of assuring him he is quite forgiven. I think I too have made some mistakes, for I was too quick to think ill of him, too unwilling to question what I knew. All in all, Harriet, the past shall remain just as it is – the past – and we shall move, Lord Galsworthy and I, into a brighter, happier future together."

Harriet sighed happily, handing her bonnet and her gloves to the butler before making her way inside. "I am truly happy for you, my dear sister," she said as they hurried up the staircase towards the drawing room, looking forward to a tea tray and a blazing fire by which they might warm their toes, for the wind had been especially cold that afternoon. "I have no doubt Father will wish to marry me off next summer, however, so I must hope that he is as considerate of me as he has been of you!"

Marianne smiled. "I think Father's view on such matters has changed considerably this last fortnight," she replied thoughtfully. "I certainly have seen him changed. In being open with him, I found that he was not angry nor irritated with me, as I had feared. Instead, he listened and accepted what I had to say, taking careful consideration of it. I am quite sure that, when your time comes, Harriet, Father will be a good deal more obliging."

Harriet chuckled. "I do hope so." Stepping into the drawing room, both ladies stopped dead, astonished to see Lord Henry shaking their father's hand.

"Lord Henry," Marianne managed to stammer, trying

to remember her manners in the face of such a surprise. She had not known he had been planning to call and, having barely had more than a single conversation with him in this last week, due to her outings with Lord Galsworthy, it was now something of an astonishment to see him standing here with her father.

"Do excuse me, Miss Weston," Lord Henry said, coming towards them, and bowing to them both. "I was just taking my leave."

"Do not let our presence chase you from here," Harriet said hastily, fearing that they were being rude in some way, but Lord Henry simply shook his head.

"No, indeed, I truly was just about to take my leave," he insisted merrily. "I will be seeing you both at my Ball, I hope?"

"Of course," Marianne replied just as Harriet said the same. "Thank you again for the invitation, Lord Henry."

He bowed and excused himself, quitting the room and leaving her and her sister to look towards their father, who was smiling quite brightly.

"My dear girls, do come in," their father said, gesturing to the chairs by the fire. "You will want a tea tray, I have no doubt! I will ring for one." As he did so, he held out his other hand to Marianne who came over to him at once, her heart beating a little faster with a sudden, inexplicable tension.

"Marianne," her father began, taking her hand in his. "Tell me, has Lord Galsworthy proposed to you yet?"

A deep flush crept up Marianne's neck and went into her cheeks. "Father," she began, trying to find a way to explain. "I believe he was going to recently, but we were interrupted. I am quite sure it will occur within the next few days."

Lord Bridgestone frowned at this, squeezing her hand gently before letting it fall. "I have not yet spoken to the gentleman, as I said I would, as you promised me that things were improving greatly with him."

"As they are," Marianne promised, suddenly a little afraid. "Why do you ask, Father?"

He gestured for her to sit down and Harriet rose to take the tea tray from the maid, sending her away almost at once. Harriet began to pour the tea, allowing Lord Bridgestone to speak to Marianne uninterrupted.

"Lord Henry has been particularly attentive towards you of late," he began quietly. "I have noticed his ardour and his insistent desire to know you better, Marianne."

Marianne blinked, a little surprised at this. "Father, Lord Henry has not come to call upon me for some days now. I believe he knows that I am being courted by Lord Galsworthy and does not wish to interfere."

"Be that as it may," Lord Bridgestone continued in a hard voice, "I have very little intention of insisting that you marry the gentleman you are betrothed to when it appears that he simply will not propose. Therefore, I have agreed that Lord Henry may court you, should you wish it."

Marianne's stomach dropped, a heavy weight settling inside her belly and sending a flood of nausea up her throat.

"That is why Lord Henry was here," Lord Bridge-stone explained, taking Marianne's silence for surprise. "He came to beg of me to allow him permission to court you, Marianne. He spoke so well that I could hardly refuse him, especially when he mentioned..." Trailing off, Lord Bridgestone shook his head, now appearing a little uneasy."

"When he mentioned...?" Marianne looked back at her father steadily, a knot of fear tightening in her belly.

"Yes, well," her father coughed, clearing his throat. "Lord Henry made an excellent point about how a long time away from England, in another hot country, no less, can often put a gentleman quite out of sorts."

Marianne exchanged glances with her sister, who was frowning heavily at their father.

"What do you mean, Father?" Harriet asked, sounding more than a little confused. "Out of sorts? Do you mean to say that you believe Lord Galsworthy's evident lack of willingness to propose is due to his time in India?"

Marianne felt herself grow a little angry at the suggestion. "Father, as much as I am obliged to Lord Henry for his suggestions, I hardly think he is any position to give such opinions," she stated firmly. "Lord Galsworthy is not at all ill, nor even 'out of sorts' as you suggest. He is quite himself, I assure you."

Her father shook his head, however, evidently not quite certain that Marianne's opinion was of greater worth than Lord Henry's. Her anger grew steadily, driven by her frustration with Lord Henry's conversation with her father, which was neither required nor wanted. For whatever reason, her father was greatly taken with the gentleman – most likely because he was charming, polite and amicable, whilst Lord Galsworthy was quiet, reserved and had certainly left Lord Bridgestone with a good many questions when it came to his lack of willingness to propose! Marianne, however, did not care for Lord Henry's opinions, nor for the man himself, not in any way. She certainly considered him a close acquaintance and, up until this moment, had been glad of his friendship. Now, however, she had no intention of marrying herself off to Lord Henry, no matter how much he might desire it.

"Marianne, I must tell you that Lord Henry was in Lord Galsworthy's townhouse recently – evidently calling on the gentleman – and discovered a letter lying on the gentleman's study desk. I do not condone what he did in reading the letter, which was not meant for him of course, but I am grateful that he came to me to tell me what was within."

Marianne clenched her fists in her lap, trying her best to keep herself calm. "What did it say, Father?"

"It said," Lord Bridgestone continued, leaning forward in an almost conspiratorial manner, "that Lord Galsworthy would be returning to his estate with the utmost haste. Do you not see what is occurring, Marianne? The gentleman is doing what he has done before. He is leaving London, just as he left for India."

Trying to think clearly and calmly without allowing her anger to cause her to speak harshly, Marianne drew in a long, steadying breath, seeing Harriet's eyes flicker with sympathy.

"Father, Lord Galsworthy will return to his estate once we are engaged," she said firmly. "I have every expectation that he will do so. It makes perfect sense and, for what it is worth, Lord Henry ought not to be reading any correspondence that is not his own." She did not know what Lord Henry was thinking, quite taken aback by the gentleman's conduct. To have him behave with such crass rudeness and arrogance quite astonished her, and she felt entirely grateful that she had never allowed herself to truly consider him. There was no affection for the man, no fondness, no sense of longing. All of which she felt for Lord Galsworthy and, had they not been interrupted the day at the art gallery, Marianne was quite sure that they would have been officially and publicly engaged by now.

Lord Bridgestone shook his head again, rising to his feet and muttering something under his breath about never quite managing to please his daughters. Harriet's lips twitched and Marianne felt her anger begin to dissipate upon seeing it, her heart softening as she realized that her father was only doing what he thought was best for her.

"Father," she said quietly. "I know that you want me to be happy and content and I am truly grateful for that consideration. Allow me to assure you that, after all that has passed between myself and Lord Galsworthy, I am quite certain that he will propose and that, within the month, I will be wed and settled."

"Are you sure that is what you want, Marianne?"

Lord Bridgestone turned to face her, his eyes a little narrowed as he studied her carefully.

"You must be certain," he continued sternly. "Lord Henry is also a gentleman of fine character and I know that you have enjoyed his acquaintance. Think carefully on it, my dear. You have time to decide, of course, for I do not think that we will see Lord Henry until his Ball in three days' time."

Marianne wanted to assure her father that yes, she was quite certain that she would refuse Lord Henry, if he asked to court her, but seeing her sister's warning look, she simply inclined her head and promised that yes, she would consider the matter. It was quite apparent that her father was a little frustrated and certainly confused over her change in feeling towards both Lord Galsworthy and Lord Henry, and to continue the conversation any further at the present time might make things all the worse.

"Thank you, my dear," Lord Bridgestone said with evident relief. "That is all I want to hear. Now, if you will excuse me, I have some correspondence that requires my attention."

Marianne smiled and waited until their father had left the room before practically exploding onto her sister. She railed at Lord Henry as though he were in the room, letting her frustration and anger evidence itself through both words and gestures. Harriet bore it all quietly, nodding in agreement at times, until Marianne finally felt herself grow tired, her emotions all released.

"I quite agree, my dear sister," Harriet said softly. "You need not worry. I am quite sure that Lord Henry will understand when you explain it all to him – although I confess, I am surprised that he did not speak to you first before going to Father."

Marianne sat back down in her chair and picked up her tea cup, considering this for a moment. "Indeed," she murmured, fully aware that this was, in fact, rather strange behaviour from a gentleman. The more she thought of it, the more she found herself beginning to dislike Lord Henry intensely. It was as though she had become the only thing he wished to possess and, even though it was quite obvious that he could not have what he wanted, he was attempting to move heaven and earth in order to manipulate the situation into his favour. The charm, the smiles, the amicability all began to fade as she let her thoughts linger on him, now beginning to see the manipulation, the arrogance and the selfish ambition that lay beneath. She shuddered involuntarily, thinking that she ought to write to Lord Galsworthy and inform him of this news so that he would not hear of it from anyone else and think her fickle in her affections. They had continued to exchange letters almost daily and she had come to look forward to his correspondence, knowing to expect one from him very soon.

"I had best write a note to him," she said, getting up from her chair so as to go to the writing desk. "I think –"

The scratch at the door stopped her and, on answering it, she was handed a note, which, to her surprise, did not have his usual seal. There was wax, yes, but no seal.

"That is most unusual," she said to herself. "Galsworthy always puts his seal on his letters." She saw Harriet glancing up at her but dismissed the thought quickly. Perhaps he had been eager to have the letter sent to her and had thus forgotten to do such a thing. Shrugging inwardly, she broke the seal and read it quickly, feeling her heart begin to sink as she took it in.

"Marianne!" Harriet exclaimed, rising quickly from her chair, and coming to take Marianne's hand. "You are ashen! Goodness, whatever is the matter? Come and sit down, quickly."

"He – he is leaving," Marianne whispered, looking at the letter again and struggling to accept what it said. "It is as Lord Henry said to Father. Lord Galsworthy has chosen to return to his estate and does not know when he will return to London. It may very well be after the little Season!" One hand covered her mouth as she struggled to contain herself, the other hand crumpling up the letter. Her sister helped her into a chair and Marianne felt herself grow suddenly weak, as though she might be about to faint. Lord Galsworthy was doing just as he had done before, he was trying to escape from her, trying to run from their impending marriage. She had been quite taken in. There was no-one as big a fool as she.

"He is not who I believed him to be," she gasped, her breathing ragged as Harriet tugged the letter from her hand and read it. "Oh, Harriet, what have I done? What shall I do?"

Harriet looked back at her wordlessly with eyes that were filled with sorrow. "I do not know, Marianne," she said helplessly. "Can it be true? Can he really be turning his back on you now?"

Marianne felt tears come to her eyes but did not dash them away. Her heart was quite broken and she allowed them to fall without attempting to hold them back. Lord Galsworthy's promises lay shattered on the floor at her feet, along with the remains of her heart. She felt completely and utterly broken.

CHAPTER FIFTEEN

*P*hilip was thinking hard. He was due to pen a letter to Miss Weston, as had become their habit of late, but he could not quite think what to say. His heart was so filled with such a great depth of emotion for her that to try to put it into words seemed almost impossible.

If only he had been able to propose to her yesterday afternoon, then mayhap the words would come more easily! As it stood, he was caught between memory and regret, truly delighted with just how open she had been to receiving his attentions and how frustrated he was that he had not been able to continue with them, due to the arrival of the other visitors in the gallery. Goodness, she had been practically begging him to kiss her again so that she might respond accordingly! That particular thought sent a shock of heat straight through him, leaving him a little breathless. He knew he was quite unable to turn from her and would have taken her in his arms again and kissed her until both of them were gasping for breath, had it not been that they had been interrupted. He felt so many things for her, but the truth was slowly becoming apparent to him the longer he dwelt on it: he cared for Miss Weston.

It was not just a fondness, it was not just an affection, but rather there was something a good deal more profound filling his heart. He could not remove his thoughts from her, found himself longing to be in her company again, when he had only bid her goodbye a few short hours ago. There was no-one like Miss Weston, he was quite sure of it. She brought such joy, such happiness to his life that he could not imagine what his life would entail were she to step away from him. How glad he was to know that their betrothal was something they were both beginning to appreciate. To propose to her would mean the banns would be called, the preparations begun and in three short weeks, they would be man and wife.

Philip could think of nothing better.

Picking up his quill, he considered for another moment before beginning to write, letting his heart speak through his words.

And then, there came a knock at the door, interrupting him entirely. Letting out a frustrated sigh, Philip called for the butler to enter, rather surprised to see him entering with a card in his hand.

"It is rather late for visitors, is it not?" he murmured as the butler held the card out to him, appearing to be a little perplexed himself.

"Indeed it is, my lord," the butler agreed with a shake of his head. "But the gentleman is quite insistent. He states that it is of the greatest urgency and no matter how much I tried to tell him that you were busy and not to be disturbed, he would not leave the house."

Philip frowned, turning the card over in his hand and wondering what on earth had possessed Lord Henry to come to his home so late in the evening. There was no particular urgency, he was quite sure, even though that was what the gentleman himself had stated.

"What should I do, my lord?" the butler asked, waiting for Philip's guidance.

Letting out a long, heavy sigh, Philip waved a hand. "I will see him, although it will be brief," he said, resigning himself to the fact that he would have to see Lord Henry, even though he did not much want to. "Do not bring up a tray or any sort of refreshments. That will not be required."

The butler inclined his head. "Of course, my lord. Do excuse me."

Philip watched him go before setting down his quill and removing the letter he was in the middle of writing to Miss Weston. He set it carefully into his desk drawer, thinking to finish it off once Lord Henry had left. His twist of nervousness left him in no doubt that he was feeling rather anxious about the gentleman's strange appearance at his home. He knew from talking to Miss Weston, that whilst she had always appreciated Lord Henry's company, she did not feel anything particular for him. That had come as something of a relief, for he had feared, at one time, that he was removing Miss Weston from the gentleman she loved. To know that it was not so and that Miss Weston simply saw Lord Henry as a close acquaintance brought Philip ongoing relief.

"Lord Henry Redmond."

Philip rose from his seat as the man came inside, displeased to see the arrogant smile on the gentleman's face as he greeted Philip. There was no expression of concern or worry, which meant that the story about having some sort of news to share with Philip had been nothing more than a fabrication, which he had impressed upon Philip's butler repeatedly until the poor man had no choice but to go to his master and mention Lord Henry's presence.

"What can I do for you, Lord Henry?" Philip asked, sitting back down and feeling himself growing eager to bring this conversation to as swift an end as he could.

Lord Henry remained standing, folding his arms over his chest. "You are not going to ask me to sit?"

"No," Philip replied at once, not feeling so much as a stab of guilt at his rudeness. "This conversation must be a short one, Lord Henry, for I have much to get on with."

Lord Henry chuckled. "Of course. You will soon be beginning preparations for your wedding, I imagine."

Something in his tone made Philip bristle and he did not immediately reply.

Still laughing, Lord Henry let his gaze travel around the room before resting it again on Philip.

"What is it that you came here for, Lord Henry?" Philip asked, determined to get the truth from the gentleman and more than eager for the man to stop wasting Philip's precious time. The letter to Miss Weston was still unfinished and he wanted to send it to her just as soon as he could.

"Well," Lord Henry began, looking quite at his ease.

"I'm afraid, Galsworthy, that I come with some rather disappointing news. I am sure you will understand in time, of course, but I'm afraid it will sting initially."

Philip resisted the urge to roll his eyes, choosing to lean back in his chair and fold his hands in his lap.

"You think me foolish, I can see," Lord Henry continued airily, "but it is all quite true, I assure you."

"What is true?" Philip asked, sighing heavily with irritation. "What is it you are talking about, Redmond?"

Lord Henry grinned, his eyes glinting darkly. "I have just come from Lord Bridgestone's home, Lord Galsworthy." He paused again and Philip had to resist the urge to rise from his chair, grasp Lord Henry by the collar and shake him until he decided to speak a good deal more quickly.

"You are not interested as to why I was at Lord Bridgestone's home?" Lord Henry asked softly. "Either that or you are determined not to appear interested. You ought to be, you know, particularly as it concerns Marianne."

Every muscle in Philip's body tightened at once, his hands twisting together as he forced himself to contain the anger that burned like a fire deep within him.

"Her name is Miss Weston," he said firmly through clenched teeth. "And no, Lord Henry, it does not interest me in any way as to why you visited Lord Bridgestone. I do not care in the least."

"Oh, but you should," Lord Henry replied with a broad smile. "Especially since her father has given me permission to court the girl."

Philip laughed, despite the pain that sliced through

him at this news. "I do not care what Lord Bridgestone has done," he replied, all too aware that he had given the gentleman a rather unfavourable impression of himself ever since he had returned from England. "There is nothing that concerns me in this." He trusted Marianne, knew that she was not interested in Lord Henry's attentions in any way. Sitting back in his chair, he forced himself to take on a nonchalant appearance, seeing the way that Lord Henry's eyes flickered, the smile beginning to fade from his face. It was quite obvious that he had convinced the gentleman that there was nothing in his news that frightened him nor set him back from his course of proposing to Miss Weston. No, nothing Lord Henry could say or do would ever prevent him from –

"What a shame, then, that I left Miss Marianne Weston in a state of distress," Lord Henry murmured, tilting his head just a little. "After all, knowing that you are to return to your estate without a word to her must be, at this very moment, breaking her heart asunder."

Philip frowned deeply. He wanted to ask, of course, what Lord Henry was talking about, but felt the urge to remain entirely silent overwhelm him. He would not give the gentleman what he so evidently desired.

"It was rather easy to send one of my messenger boys into your home," Lord Henry continued with a slight shrug. "To find the letter which you had every intention of sending to your steward was a boon that I cannot ever express my gratitude."

Sitting up straight, Philip's breath caught as he began to search for the letter he had not yet sent, having intended to do so by the end of the week once he had proposed to Miss Weston.

"You need not search for it," Lord Henry chuckled as though it was all some sort of wonderful joke. "I have it in my possession, as proof of your intentions, should Miss Weston question it."

"How dare you?" Philip breathed, getting to his feet, and feeling an almost murderous rage come over him. "You break into my home and steal –"

"*I* did nothing of the sort," Lord Henry interrupted with a dark look. "It was just by chance that this letter fell into my hands, I assure you." His lips curved into a menacing smile and Philip felt his gut twist with rage.

"On top of which," Lord Henry continued, almost airily, "I have quite convinced Lord Bridgestone that you have not proposed to Miss Weston as yet, simply because you are quite unwell. Therefore, he considers you no longer suitable to be his daughter's husband."

"Unwell?" Philip repeated harshly. "What are you talking about, Lord Henry?"

The gentleman shrugged. "You know how it is," he replied with a smile. "One spends too much time in the sun, then one can become quite unstable for a time. Indeed, Lord Galsworthy, it is not your fault that you have become so poorly and I insist that you look after yourself." His smile spread and Philip found himself moving around his desk towards the gentleman, his intention solely fixed on removing that dreadful smile from his face.

"Now, now," Lord Henry said at once, putting up both his hands in a gesture of defense. "What would your dear lady think if I was to appear at her door, battered and bruised by your hand?"

Philip stopped dead, his breathing heavy. "You are nothing but a liar and a charlatan," he stated angrily. "What makes you think that I will not simply go to Miss Weston's side and explain everything to her?"

Lord Henry chuckled, lowering his hands. "Because, my dear fellow, the game is won. Lord Bridgestone has decided against you. *I* am to be Miss Weston's husband, just as I have always intended."

"But why her?" Philip asked, his hands curling into fists. "Why must you try for Miss Weston when you know she is already engaged?"

A slow smile spread across Lord Henry's face. "Because, old boy," he began as though they were very old friends discussing something quite trivial, "I always get what I want, no matter what I have to do to gain it. I have set my sights on Miss Weston and therefore, regardless of whether or not she is already betrothed, I will have her. She is witty, bright, clever, beautiful and a rich daughter of a Viscount. I hear she comes with a hefty dowry and that only adds to my regard for her." He laughed aloud, the sound becoming menacing, galling Philip all the more.

"You do not care one jot for Miss Weston," he shouted, advancing towards Lord Henry again. "And nor does she care for you. I will explain everything to her. I will not remove myself from her presence until she finally understands and accepts me. Do you hear me, Redmond? You will not win in this. Miss Weston is mine and mine alone. I love her. You cannot take her from me. You will not succeed."

"Oh, but I will," Lord Henry replied lazily, as though he had not heard any of Philip's passionate speech. "You, however, will be quite unable to do anything about it. You will not be able to write to her, to speak to her, or even to remove yourself from this place. The deed will be done before you can rise from your bed."

"You are talking rot!" Philip roared, making to grab at Lord Henry. Out of the corner of his eye, he saw a flash of something metallic which caught the light and, in that moment, the truth of what Lord Henry intended to do became clear to him. He twisted away, just as the report of the gun filled the room. Pain lanced him and he staggered back, only to see Lord Henry hide the pistol back within his coat.

"Do excuse me, Lord Galsworthy," Lord Henry murmured, making his way to the door. Philip tried to call out, tried to go after him, but found he could not even speak a single word. The pain was increasing with every moment, a soft moaning coming from his lips as he tried to move from where he lay.

"Your master does not wish to be disturbed," he heard Lord Henry say loudly as the sound of a key turning in the lock met his ears. "He has had some distressing news and wishes to be left alone for the rest of the evening."

No! Philip tried to say, hearing the word echo only in his mind as he rolled to one side, feeling warm blood begin to stream down his arm. *Help me.*

The sound of Lord Henry's footsteps began to echo

down the corridor, followed by the butler's, who was evidently making sure that the gentleman found his way back towards the front door. Philip felt blackness begin to creep towards him, attempting to take him away from the present. Squeezing his eyes closed, he gritted his teeth and tried to find some sort of strength. The shock of what had occurred was filling him with weakness, dragging him down into the depths, but Philip was determined not to give in.

"Marianne."

Finally, he was able to speak. Even if her name was whispered through dry, heavy lips. Turning over onto his side, he forced himself to push up onto his knees with his one good hand, the other hanging uselessly by his side. The pain intensified but Philip did not give into it, his mind filling with thoughts of Marianne. She was the only thing he could hold onto whilst the rest of his world swirled in a haze of pain.

Somehow, he managed to grasp onto the arm of a chair and pull himself up to standing, although he almost toppled right into the chair itself such was the weakness in his limbs. Drawing in a breath, he tried to shout for help, feeling his head begin to spin with the effort of it.

"My lord?" Philip let out a groan of relief, feeling the last of his strength begin to die away. "My lord!" The butler rattled the door handle, only to find it locked. "Can you unlock the door, my lord?" he called, but Philip could see no key.

"I don't have it," he managed to say, although he could not tell whether or not the butler heard him. Looking down at his arm with heavy-lidded eyes, he took in the dark red stain that was making its way down his sleeve, realizing just how badly he had been shot. Had he not seen the pistol, had he not twisted to one side when he did, then would the bullet have pierced his heart rather than his shoulder? There was a lot of blood coming from the wound which was perhaps the reason he felt so faint.

Unable to hold himself upright any longer, Philip let himself collapse into the chair, his head lolling back against it. There was, by this time, the sound of shouting and scuffling at the door, but it all seemed to be so very far away, growing all the more distant with almost every moment. Philip felt his eyes close, letting out a heavy sigh as he finally gave himself up to the pain, the distress that Lord Henry had caused burning through him. Somehow, he had to find the strength to write to her, to go to her, to tell her that everything Lord Henry had done was nothing more than a lie – but with each passing second, Philip felt himself grow weaker.

You, however, will be quite unable to do anything about it. You will not be able to write to her, to speak to her, or even to remove yourself from this place. The deed will be done before you can rise from your bed.

The words Lord Henry had sneered at him just before he'd shot Philip now made sense. This was Redmond's aim. To remove Philip's strength, and mayhap his very life, before he could reach out to Marianne. Try as he might, Philip could not even move himself from his chair, could not even open his eyes as the door to his study opened with a loud cracking sound, followed swiftly by hurried feet.

"Good gracious, he has been shot!"

Philip heard his butler speaking but found that he could say nothing in response. He could not move, he could not open his eyes, he could do absolutely nothing.

"Send for the doctor," the butler continued in a voice filled with anxiety. "Then we must get the master to his bedchamber. Hurry now."

Philip tried to speak, wanted to tell the butler to fetch Miss Weston, or to at least inform her of what had occurred, but his strength was gone. The blackness came for him again and this time Philip gave himself up to it entirely, unable to do anything else but sink into its welcoming embrace.

CHAPTER SIXTEEN

*O*pening his eyes was impossible, Philip was sure of it.

"Come now, my lord," a brusque voice stated firmly. "You must do so at once. Your poor mother is quite distraught."

"Galsworthy?"

His mother was here, Philip could tell. Her voice was cracked and broken, evidencing her concern. He wanted to reach for her, to take her hand and tell her that he was quite all right, but he could not.

"Try again, my lord," the gruff voice insisted. "Come now, you were only shot in the shoulder! Yes, you may have lost a good deal of blood but a hearty young gentleman like yourself ought to be able to deal with it quite easily. Make an effort, my lord!"

Philip wanted to shout that he *was* making an effort, that he *was* doing all he could to prove to his mother that he was recovering, but the strength it took to do such a simple thing seemed almost beyond him. Finally, he

managed to crack open one eye, much to the delight of
the doctor, who was the man Philip presumed was now
bending over him. Opening both eyes, he blinked to clear
his vision, seeing his mother rush towards him and take
his hand.

"Oh, Philip," she whispered, referring to him by his
Christian name which she very rarely did. "You have
returned to us."

"Just as I said," the doctor replied with an air of satisfaction that Philip disliked intensely. "You may wish to
sit up in a few minutes, my lord. It is better for you to try
to rebuild your strength as quickly as you can, for to lie in
bed can often bring more harm than good. I have seen too
many ladies, in particular, take to their beds in a bout of
weakness, only to spend the rest of their years there. I
strongly discourage you from doing the same."

Finding the doctor more and more irritating, Philip
tried to push himself up to sitting, only to let out a groan
of pain at the streak of agony that ran through his left
side.

"Careful now," the doctor said at once, finally
showing a little concern. "As I said, Lord Galsworthy, you
have been shot. Whilst I encourage you to rise from your
bed as soon as you can, you must not be foolhardy."

"I am not being foolhardy," Philip whispered, his
voice hoarse. Trying to sit up a good deal more carefully,
he finally managed to do so, feeling almost worn out from
the effort.

"Oh, Galsworthy," his mother whispered, her face
paper white and her hand grasping his tightly. "Whatever
happened?"

Philip shook his head, the memory of what had occurred coming back to him with a startling swiftness. "A particular gentleman wanted me removed entirely from society's presence for a time so that he might marry Miss Weston in my stead."

His mother gasped, one hand at her mouth, her light hazel eyes wide with horror.

"I must go to her," he said knowing that he had no strength with which to do so. "Or write to her, at least."

"To Miss Weston?" his mother queried. "Oh, but of course, Galsworthy. I can fetch some paper for you at once."

Philip made to thank her, only for the words to die on his lips. "Wait, Mama," he said as the butler brought in a tray evidently meant for Lady Galsworthy. Philip watched as the butler, at the behest of Lady Galsworthy, brought it over to him at once, setting it down carefully with relief etched across his expression.

"May I say, my lord, just how glad I am to see you recovered," the butler said with a small bow. "And may I apologize for not coming to your aid sooner."

Philip shook his head, ignoring the pain that ran down his side as he did so. "It was not your fault in any way," he assured him, grateful for such loyal staff. "Were it not for you, then I might very well have bled —"

He stopped dead, hearing his mother's strangled sob.

"What I mean to say is," he continued, "is to say thank you."

The butler bowed again. "Of course, my lord."

Lady Galsworthy handed Philip a cup of tea and he

took a sip, watching her buttering a piece of toast for him and feeling a good deal more himself.

"Also," he continued, directing his gaze back towards the butler. "I want you to do something for me at once," Philip continued, feeling strength begin to flow into him as his determination grew. "Apparently a messenger boy managed to make his way into my home and stole something from my desk."

The butler blanched and Philip immediately held up one hand.

"I do not blame you for this, so you need not look so afraid," he said quickly. "I simply want to ensure that the lock to my study is changed at once and that each and every servant is asked whether or not they saw this boy entering my home and that they are on their guard should such a thing to occur again. Each of the doors and windows are to be locked up tightly, except for entering and exiting the house. I will not have Lord Henry attempt anything further." He saw the butler nod and drew in a long breath. "Finally, the staff are to be told, in unequivocal terms, that none of them are to say a word about my injury nor my recovery, not to any other living soul outside this house," he finished as the butler nodded again. "It is vital that they say nothing and, should I hear that news has somehow got out into society, the person responsible will be let go without warning and without reference."

"I quite understand, my lord," the butler replied firmly. "I shall do so at once – and I will bring you another tray, Lady Galsworthy."

"Take it to the drawing room," Philip stated as the

doctor looked on approvingly. "I shall dress and join you there, Mama."

"Are you quite sure?" she asked, one hand at her heart as she looked towards the doctor, who appeared to be quite pleased over Philip's determination.

Philip nodded, biting into his toast. "I shall eat and then join you below," he promised, knowing that he would have to find his strength if he was to make his way back towards Miss Weston before Lord Henry could convince her that Philip truly had gone back to his estate for good.

"Very well," his mother replied doubtfully, letting go of his hand. "If you are sure, Galsworthy."

"More than sure," he replied, with as much fervour as he could. "I will be with you in a few minutes, Mama."

It took Philip a good hour or so before he was quite able to make his way to the drawing room, disliking intensely the weakness of his limbs. Even with Gibbs' assistance, he was not properly dressed, given that his arm was in a sling which he wore about his neck, but the loose shirt and waistcoat would have to do. He now found himself struggling to put one foot in front of the other as he walked into the drawing room.

His mother rose to her feet at once, coming to help him, but Philip shook his head. "Thank you, Mama, I am quite all right," he stated through gritted teeth. "Might you ring for some sort of refreshment? I find that I am still quite hungry."

Lady Galsworthy saw a maid passing and sent her away with instructions, before lowering herself back into her chair with her eyes fixed on Philip. Somehow, he managed to maneuver himself into his chair, only once knocking his elbow as he did so, which sent waves of pain all through him. Gritting his teeth, he closed his eyes and waited for it to pass. The doctor, unfortunately, had found it necessary to cauterize the wound with a hot poker, after digging the ball out of his flesh, although Philip himself had not yet seen what the state of his shoulder was like for himself. It was painful indeed but, at least it was not bleeding any longer. The pain would pass in time and his shoulder would heal. Now if only his strength would return completely!

Two maids appeared with trays, setting more tea down in front of Lady Galsworthy, and a tray piled high with all kinds of delicacies in front of Philip. He thanked them and waited until they had left before gesturing to his mother to eat something.

"I thank you," Lady Galsworthy said, her eyes fixed on him. "Tell me, Galsworthy, did I truly hear you say that it was Lord Henry Redmond who is responsible for all of this?"

"I did," Philip replied grimly. "That is why I do not wish you to get the paper and ink so that I might write to Miss Weston, Mama. I think that, even should I try to write to Miss Weston, Lord Henry might attempt to prevent her from either reading or even seeing it. No, I have a better plan in mind."

She nodded, her face still quite ashen. "I cannot quite comprehend this, Galsworthy," she breathed, her hand still shaking just a little as she poured the tea. "You could have been killed."

"Thankfully, I saw the pistol and dodged it as best I could," Philip replied with a bleak smile. "I did not think that he would ever do something as terrible as this, simply to gain what he wants. That is the thing with Lord Henry, I think, Mama. He has always been filled with his own sense of self-importance, arrogant enough to believe he ought to be given anything and everything he deserves."

"But what of Miss Weston?" his mother asked as the sound of raised voices began to tumble towards them from the hallway. "How is she to know of Lord Henry's betrayal of both her and you, if you will not write to her?"

Philip paused for a moment, wondering at the commotion that was coming towards them. "I thought to go to Lord Henry's Ball, Mama."

She gasped and made to speak, only for the door to the drawing room to fly open and none other than Miss Harriet Weston to appear in the doorway, her blue eyes filled with rage. She ignored Lady Galsworthy entirely but pointed one long finger at Philip whilst the butler began to apologize over and over for not managing to prevent the young lady from finding Philip.

"Why are you returning to your estate without so much as a word to my sister?" Miss Harriet Weston shouted, her hand shaking with rage. "How dare you leave her so heartbroken?"

Philip closed his eyes for a moment, then gestured for her to come in, sending the butler away.

"Miss Weston," he said calmly. "If you will but listen, then I am quite sure that you will understand."

"She *loves* you, Lord Galsworthy!" Miss Harriet continued as though she had not heard him at all. "How can you treat her so poorly? I have been with her almost the entire night as she has cried and..." She trailed off, her hand falling to her side as her eyes went to his arm that was still held tightly in the sling. "Has something occurred, Lord Galsworthy?"

"Please," he said quietly. "Do sit down, Miss Weston. As you can see, I am not preparing to take my leave of London. That is, I am afraid, nothing more than a lie taken from the mouth of Lord Henry Redmond."

"Although it is good of you to be so distraught on your sister's behalf," Lady Galsworthy said, making Miss Weston jump as if she had only just realized that Philip's mother was also with him.

"I do not understand," Miss Weston said, seating herself carefully and studying Philip with puzzlement. "From your letter to Marianne, I thought –"

"What letter?" Philip asked, interrupting her. "I wrote no letter to her."

"A letter stating that you were leaving London for your estate and did not know when you would return," Miss Weston said in a small voice. "Marianne believed it to be from you."

Philip closed his eyes for a moment, battling the rage that threatened to overwhelm him. "No, indeed," he replied slowly. "I wrote no such thing, Miss Weston. I have never thought to turn my back on your sister. My heart is full of her and her alone."

Miss Weston seemed to accept this, nodding slowly as her eyes widened as understanding crept across her face. "Then it was Lord Henry who wrote the letter?" she queried. "My sister mumbled something about there not being any seal but she obviously did not think much of it."

"I expect that it was Lord Henry, yes," Philip agreed, gesturing to his shoulder. "As he is responsible for this also, I consider him to be a highly dangerous gentleman, determined to have whatever he has set his mind to."

Miss Weston gasped, one hand flying to her mouth.

"Tea, Miss Weston?" Lady Galsworthy asked, reaching for the spare china cup and saucer that had been meant for Philip. "It is a shock, of course, but I believe Galsworthy has an idea as to how to set it all to rights again."

"Do you, Lord Galsworthy?" Miss Weston asked at once, taking the cup from Lady Galsworthy with a slightly shaking hand. "My sister is broken hearted and I would not like her to remain in such a state if there is no truth in what she believes."

Philip smiled sadly, feeling his heart clench with the grief of knowing his betrothed was distraught over what she believed to be his lack of commitment to her. "No, nor do I wish to keep her in her distress," he replied slowly. "But Lord Henry cannot know of my recovery. His intention was to injure me so terribly as to keep me in my bed, away from his Ball and from Miss Marianne. Therefore, you may tell her that I am not away to my estate, as she has been told, and you may tell her that the letter was not from my hand, but she must not be told any more." He saw Miss Weston frown but kept his resolve steady. "Lord Henry may notice her change in attitude and may question it if she is told any more," he explained. "I believe he is at Miss Weston's side at this very moment?"

It was his expectation that Lord Henry would do his best not to be separated from Marianne in the hope that he might convince her, in her grief, that he was the better gentleman for her. His expectation was met by Miss Weston's nod of agreement.

"Then can you do as I have asked?" Philip queried, seeing the way Miss Weston frowned again. "It will be for the best, I assure you."

"But when will you see her again, to convince her that all is not as she thinks?" Lady Galsworthy asked, adding more tea to her cup. "If Lord Henry is always by her side, then how can you hope to avoid him?"

Philip chuckled darkly. "I intend to put in an appearance at his Ball, Mama, where he will be caught up with his guests. I intend to confront him there, to show Miss Marianne that he is not a man who can be trusted."

"I believe she knows that already," Miss Weston murmured, rising from her chair. "I must go to her at once. I will do as you ask, Lord Galsworthy, and look forward to the Ball tomorrow evening so that all may be set right. I only want to see my sister happy again."

"As do I," Philip assured her with a smile. "Thank you, Miss Weston. Until tomorrow."

"Until tomorrow," she replied before leaving the room to return to her sister.

$\mathcal{M}$arianne tensed visibly as Lord Henry laughed loudly, the sound of his voice filling the drawing room where she sat. Her father had invited Lord Henry to dinner that evening, much to Marianne's chagrin, and of course Lord Henry had agreed at once. She had been forced to suffer through his long conversations, although she had made no attempt to respond, or even smile for that matter. Harriet had done her best to fill in where Marianne could not, although, from what Marianne could see, there was something in Harriet's expression that she could not quite make out. It was as if Harriet had something which she was desperate to reveal to her but could not, given their present company. There was a brightness to her eyes that Marianne could not quite understand, and an almost desperate countenance as though she was eager for the dinner to come to an end.

But, then again, mayhap Harriet was as unhappy with Lord Henry's company as she was.

"I think the Ball will go wonderfully well," Lord Henry said grandly, his eyes darkening as he looked towards Marianne. "I am sure that my many guests will enjoy the evening and all that comes with it. It will give them a good deal to gossip over, I am quite sure."

Marianne's breath caught, her stomach twisting horribly.

Lord Bridgestone chuckled. "I can see you are a gentleman who acts quickly when it comes to what he wants."

"Indeed, I am," Lord Henry murmured, his eyes still fixed on Marianne. "I always know what will bring me happiness."

Marianne felt as though she might cast up her accounts right there in front of them all, feeling decidedly queasy.

"Come now," Harriet interrupted, getting to her feet. "Enough conversation. Might I play for us all?" She made to move towards the pianoforte, only for Lord Henry to rise to his feet.

"Might I be so bold as to ask for a turn about the room with you, Miss Weston?" he asked, directing his question towards Marianne. "There are a few more things I wish to discuss with you and, as yet, we have not had the time."

Marianne looked up at him but did not move from her chair. "I confess that I am rather tired, Lord Henry," she said in a dull voice. "In fact, I thought to retire to bed."

He pressed one hand to his heart in mock horror. "Surely not, my lady!" he exclaimed as she caught sight of her father's deepening frown. "Might you not walk with me for a short time?"

"Do go with Lord Henry, Marianne," her father interjected, getting to his feet and gesturing for her to go with the gentleman. "Why do you not take him to the library? I know that you will be greatly impressed with the number of books within, Lord Henry."

"It may even exceed my own!" Lord Henry replied with a chuckle before offering Marianne his arm. "Come then, my dear lady. Let us go."

Marianne cast a look towards Harriet who was standing helplessly by the fire, her eyes ablaze with frustration and anger.

"I can attend you," Harriet began, only for their father to cut her off with a loud, booming laugh.

"I think we can give them a few minutes, my dear," he chuckled as though Harriet were being much too ridiculous. "We will join you there in a moment, Lord Henry, of course."

"Of course," the gentleman grinned, inclining his head before looking towards Marianne. She had no other recourse but to take his proffered arm, knowing that to refuse would be more than a little rude, and would certainly bring about the wrath of her father. Trying to convince herself that to speak to the gentleman alone was, perhaps, a blessing – for she could then tell him directly that, even should he wish to marry her with a desperation that could not be withstood, she would have no other choice but to refuse him. To be his wife was not something she could even contemplate, not when she still loved Lord Galsworthy with almost everything she had.

She had realized her love for him in the midst of her grief, knowing that she would not feel as truly broken as she did, had she not a true, deep affection for the gentleman.

"Very well," she murmured with a small sigh, accepting his arm and walking with him to the door. As they made their way towards the library, the silence grew thick about them both, making Marianne's heart quicken with a deep, unsettling dread.

"You are very contemplative, my dear," Lord Henry murmured with a good deal of tenderness in his voice. "I do hope you will not be so downhearted come the morrow."

She lifted her chin. "I confess, Lord Henry, I am not certain I shall be able to attend tomorrow evening, given the state of my melancholy."

He laughed harshly, the sound seeming to fill the house, and her very being along with it. Shuddering, she looked away from him and tugged her hand out from his arm, which made him laugh all the more.

"Please," she said softly. "We need not put on this façade any longer, Lord Henry. I know full well that you are seeking my affections, but I tell you now that I cannot give them to you."

"Why ever not?" he retorted, spinning around to face her just as they approached the library door. "Why can you not wed me now that Lord Galsworthy has rejected you?"

Her heart cried out in pain as though he had struck her a knife blow.

"He has not rejected me," she argued, determined to stand up to him despite her knowledge that Lord

Galsworthy had done just that. "He is gone to his estate, which I well understand, given his responsibilities to the title and the fact that he has long been away from home. I am quite sure he will return just as soon as he is able."

Lord Henry snorted. "I hardly think so," he sneered, his face growing all the more terrible as he mocked her. "You must face the truth, Miss Weston. He is gone from you, just as he ran from you before. Why do you waste your time on a gentleman such as that, when one who is all the more suitable for you stands directly in front of you?"

"I know full well that you consider yourself to be such a gentleman," she replied, revulsion continuing to fill her as she saw how he sneered at her. "But I could never marry you, Lord Henry, not even if you begged me on your knees. I would rather remain alone and become a spinster than wed you."

His expression darkened and for a moment Marianne was afraid he might strike her, such was the anger on his face. Then, to her ever increasing horror, he dragged her into his arms and attempted to kiss her.

She fought him with everything she had, her mind screaming in fear as he tried to place his lips on hers. This was not the man she had thought Lord Henry to be, when they had first met. She had thought him amiable and considerate, and now here he was, attempting to force her into matrimony through any means he could. Flailing, she felt him push her back against the wall as though to pin her there. Using every bit of strength and courage she had, she fought his advances, one of her hands landing directly in his eye.

Lord Henry stumbled back with a yelp of pain, one hand pressed to his eye.

"You little witch!" he hissed, making to grab for her again, but Marianne dodged him easily enough, hurrying away from him.

"I will have you as my wife, Marianne!" he shouted after her as she stumbled away from him, desperate to reach the safety of her bedchamber. "No matter what you attempt, I will win in the end!"

He has gone quite mad, Marianne thought to herself as, gasping, she reached her bedchamber and flung the door open before shutting it again tightly. Leaning against it, she let herself sink to the floor, her legs growing tired and weak with the shock of what had just occurred. She did not know how long she remained there, but the tears flowed easily and she did not hold them back. Everything had turned from delight and joy into darkness and pain. Lord Galsworthy, the man she knew now that she loved desperately, had rejected her by deciding to run from her side yet again, leaving her to stand alone against the advances of Lord Henry. Lord Henry, the gentleman who had appeared to be kind, considerate and amicable and who, in fact, she had considered to be a friend, had now become her torturer, doing all he could to force her into a prison of his own making. There was no love in his advances, no considerations or genuine affection. He embodied all selfishness, all arrogance, all pride. She could never tie herself to him.

"Marianne?"

"Harriet!"

Scrambling to her feet, Marianne opened her door

carefully to see her sister standing outside it, looking at her with great anxiety in her eyes.

"Whatever happened, Marianne?" Harriet asked, immediately reaching for Marianne's hands. "Lord Henry said that you had a headache and had to retire to bed. Father did not seem to mind all that much, but I knew I had to come and see you at once. What did he do?"

"Oh, Harriet," Marianne whispered, dissolving into tears. "He is desperate to wed me and will not accept my refusal of him."

Harriet shook her head, her eyes growing angry. "There is more to Lord Henry than you know, Marianne. You must not allow him to weary you."

"I will not go to his Ball tomorrow," Marianne stated firmly, wiping the tears from her eyes. "I will have nothing more to do with him and even if Father presses me, I will not allow myself to be in his company any longer."

"Oh, but you must go!" Harriet exclaimed, astonishing Marianne entirely. "You must go to Lord Henry's Ball, Marianne. You must!"

Marianne, who had not expected this response, shook her head, feeling as though the entire world were set against her. "Why would you suggest such a thing?" she asked brokenly, pulling her hands from her sister's. "After all that has just occurred, I cannot understand why you would –"

"Lord Galsworthy will be there," Harriet replied, interrupting her.

Marianne felt her breath leave her body entirely,

going quite limp as she stared at her sister. She was forced to collapse into a seat, her heart thundering wildly and her breathing ragged.

"I know this is a shock," Harriet said, sitting down opposite her, and leaning forward in her chair. "I had meant to tell you all this afternoon, but Lord Henry was already present and so I could not do so."

Marianne could barely breathe, one hand pressed hard against her stomach as she fought to drag in air. Her mind was whirling, confused beyond measure as she looked blankly back into Harriet's eyes.

"I went to Lord Galsworthy's townhouse in the hope that he had not yet left for the country," Harriet explained as Marianne studied her sister with incomprehension. "I thought to rail at him, Marianne, for your sake. I was quite angry, I confess, but there is more to what has occurred than we know."

Blinking furiously, Marianne forced her tears back realizing that her sister had attempted to do her a great kindness. "He was still in London?"

"He *is* still in London, and will be at the Ball tomorrow evening, although you must not say so to Lord Henry," Harriet explained calmly. "Marianne, everything will become clear then, I promise you."

Marianne drew in a shaking breath, closing her eyes so as to regain her composure. "I do not understand, Harriet. Lord Galsworthy was to leave London. I saw his letter."

"No," Harriet replied firmly, shaking her head. "No, he is not to leave London. That was never the case, Marianne. That letter was not from him."

Her heart dropped to her toes and then ricocheted back up to her chest, making her gasp.

"Remember, you murmured something to yourself about there not being his usual seal on the letter," Harriet reminded her, bringing that moment back to her with full clarity. "You said something about it at the time, but I did not think you thought much of it for you simply opened the letter and then read it."

Marianne nodded slowly. "Yes, I did," she murmured, feeling the color drain from her face. "Oh, goodness, Harriet. I never once considered –"

She stopped dead, looking at her sister with confusion. "But if the letter was not from him and he now knows of it, why is he not here himself to tell it to me?"

Harriet let out a long breath. "Because, my dear sister, Lord Galsworthy is taking every precaution when it comes to you and the love you share. He will prove himself to you and, in doing so, will remove Lord Henry's hold forever. The gentleman is more dangerous than you know, Marianne."

"Lord Henry is a villain," Marianne replied with feeling, recalling how he had attempted to kiss her without even the slightest concern for her wellbeing or her reputation. "But I cannot understand what Galsworthy is doing. If he is not going to his estate, as he has said, then what has prevented him from corresponding with me? He could have written, if not visited, could he not?"

"No," Harriet replied with a sad smile. "No, Marianne, he could not. He begged me not to tell you more, for fear that your behaviour would be somewhat different in front of Lord Henry, who might notice and begin to think that his plan was going awry. Might you be able to wait until tomorrow night, my dear sister? I confess I do not know what Lord Galsworthy's exact plan is, but I am quite sure that it will all work out for the best."

"But we will not see Lord Henry until tomorrow evening," she said frowning. "Surely that means you can tell me all."

Harriet shook her head. "Father has invited him to luncheon to make up for this evening's lack of company," she said with a rueful smile. "It seems you are not to escape from him as you hoped."

Marianne let out a long, slow breath, considering what she had just been told. She was not quite sure what to make of it all, feeling as though she had been dragged from one deep emotion to the next without being able to stop for breath.

"Does he think ill of me?" she whispered, dreading the answer. "I thought the letter was from him without hesitation. I did not allow myself to even imagine that there was some sort of mistake. Truly, Harriet, I thought him leaving London as he had done before. Does that speak ill of me and my trust in him?"

Harriet leaned forward and took Marianne's hand in her own, a warm smile on her face. "You need not drag yourself over hot coals, Marianne," she stated firmly. "You have not done anything wrong. Lord Henry is the one at fault, for he has conceived all of this for his own benefit. He used Lord Galsworthy's past mistakes to try to force you apart. What Lord Henry has done far outweighs any poor consideration on your part, or lack of courage on Lord Galsworthy's part. I believe that Lord

Galsworthy now knows that he ought to have proposed to you some time ago, and regrets that he did not. That will not be the case tomorrow night, I believe. Trust me, Marianne, you need bear no guilt. Lord Galsworthy holds nothing against you, he only asks that you place your trust in him once more, knowing that he has not left you as you believed."

A peace settled across Marianne's soul, letting her draw in a long, freeing breath which seemed to chase the last of her sadness and fear away. She was not alone as she had believed. She was not rejected, for Lord Galsworthy had not turned away from her as she had thought. The love she had for him burned anew, settling into her soul. Her affection for him was returned, her love was not to go out from her towards emptiness.

"Tomorrow evening I will know everything," she stated, seeing Harriet nodding in agreement. "I can trust Lord Galsworthy, I know I can."

"And he is desperate to be by your side again," Harriet murmured, a gentle smile settling on her face. "Take courage, Marianne. All will be well, I promise you."

CHAPTER EIGHTEEN

*P*hilip climbed the staircase two at a time, the urge to hide away in the balcony rising steadily through him. He had made it into Lord Henry's Ball without being noticed by his host, which was of a great relief to him. He had never been to Lord Henry's house before and was quite sure that this property did not belong to the gentleman, given that he was considering purchasing a property in Grosvenor Square. Most likely, the gentleman was simply renting this magnificent property, simply to show off his wealth and status to any who came to call.

Anger burned in his veins but he forced it back with an effort. He could not allow himself to be hot-headed now, not when he had to take a good deal of care. Each moment had to be considered, each action well thought out. He could not allow Lord Henry to see him before the most opportune moment.

His breath caught in his chest as he laid eyes on Miss Weston, who was standing by her sister and father at the side of the ballroom. She was dressed in a pale blue gown that he was sure would highlight the beauty and color of her eyes, her fair hair tumbling from an intricate arrangement on the top of her head, down her back, in long, gentle curls. She was utterly breath-taking and the desire to go to her, to be by her side, almost overwhelmed him entirely.

Her eyes were roving about the room, looking from one guest to another, searching for someone. He knew full well that she was searching for him, happiness settling into his soul. Miss Harriet had done her duty, it seemed, else he would expect to see her standing desolately, looking as though her whole world had crumbled to the ground.

"My dear Marianne," Philip whispered to himself, his hands tightening on the rail as he saw Lord Henry bow in front of her. "You must only endure a little while longer. Then I will not be separated from you again."

Philip watched with growing anger as Lord Henry bowed again in front of Marianne before offering her his hand. It was a waltz and, for a moment, Philip thought Marianne was about to refuse, seeing the way that she glanced from one side to the other. She knew full well that the other guests in the ballroom were watching her and that even her father, Lord Bridgestone, would not be pleased if she refused Lord Henry. To turn away from Lord Henry now, in front of his guests, would be to insult him greatly. The ballroom would be alive with whispers almost at once, should she do so. Philip could not imagine all that she must be feeling, hating that she had to stand up with the very man who had brought her so much trouble, but stand up with him she did.

He could not take his eyes from her, seeing the way that she danced with Lord Henry without ever really looking at him. It was more than apparent to him that she longed to be free of Henry's embrace, her eyes still searching for him.

And then, she saw him.

Philip's heart began to race as her eyes fixed on his, broken by the turns and spins of the dance. He wanted to call out to her, wanted to beg her to come to him, but knew he could not. Instead, he simply smiled gently and held her gaze, seeing the way the corners of her mouth turned up just a little.

It was time to begin.

Stepping away from the balcony, Philip made his way down the staircase and proceeded into the ballroom, staying close to the wall. He did not want to make his presence obvious as yet, but knew that it would soon be time to confront Lord Henry in front of all his guests. He did not care about the rumours it would bring, knowing that he had to reveal Lord Henry's treachery to the *ton* in order to keep Marianne – as well as other eligible young ladies – safe from the man. His shoulder ached terribly but Philip ignored it altogether, telling himself that he could not spare even a moment's thought for his own pain.

"Lord Galsworthy!"

Putting a small smile on his face, Philip bowed towards Harriet and then greeted Lord Bridgestone who was staring at him with utter astonishment.

"Lord Galsworthy," Lord Bridgestone stuttered, clearly quite at a loss. "I thought you were – I mean, Lord Henry stated that you would be leaving London. I thought you had already returned to your estate."

"I believe he also told you that I was quite unwell," Philip replied, seeing the man look away uncomfortably. "I am not at all ill, Lord Bridgestone. It is all nothing more than a fabrication made by Lord Henry in the hope that he might separate me from your daughter."

Lord Bridgestone looked as though he did not know what to believe. "I do not quite understand, Lord Galsworthy," he replied slowly. "Lord Henry is a good man and I can hardly believe that –"

"Lord Henry shot him!" Harriet exclaimed, her hand on her father's arm. "He did so to prevent Lord Galsworthy from coming to you with the truth, Father!"

Philip saw the astonishment creep into Lord Bridgestone's expression, followed by a slight frown that betrayed the gentleman's immediate lack of belief. "I hardly think that–"

"I can show you the wound if that would persuade you," Philip interjected at once, rather more sternly than he had intended. "I am quite aware, Lord Bridgestone, that Lord Henry has done everything he can to ingratiate himself into your family in order to persuade you that he, rather than I, would be a much better gentleman for your daughter, whereas the opposite is quite true. Lord Henry is a scoundrel and nothing more. He has decided he wants to wed Miss Weston and so, therefore, has done all he can to gain her hand and your trust." Seeing that Lord Bridgestone's frown was now deepening, Philip took a breath before he continued, relieved that the gentleman appeared to be feeling a hint of anger; such was the glint in his eye. "I stand before you as hail and as hearty as any man, Lord Bridgestone. I confess that I have been foolish in turning away from your daughter when I ought to have been courting her with the urgency that I now feel. I ought to have proposed long ago and made our engagement known. Having spent time with Miss Weston, I confess that I have grown more than fond of her, Lord Bridgestone. I love her. I love her more with each day that passes which is why I simply could not allow Lord Henry to continue. Your daughter is right to tell you that the gentleman shot me for that was precisely what he did only two days ago, immediately after he came from your home. He thought to convince me to leave Miss Weston to him, stating precisely what he had told you about my supposed illness and my return to the estate. When I told him that I would not stand for it, he attempted to give me a grievous injury that, had I not turned at the last moment, would have put me near death."

Lord Bridgestone shook his head and rubbed one hand over his forehead. "I do not want to believe it," he muttered to himself, shaking his head. "And yet, it appears that I must. Lord Henry is not, then, the man I thought him."

"No, Father," Miss Harriet Weston said gently, putting one hand on her father's arm. "He is not. Lord Galsworthy loves Marianne, I know he does. And Marianne loves him, Father. You cannot separate them now. Once Marianne knows all, then I know she will choose Lord Galsworthy."

"A thousand times over, I do."

Philip turned sharply, seeing Miss Marianne Weston standing just behind him with Lord Henry now making his way towards her, elbowing his way through the crowd. Evidently, she had been listening to what Philip had said to Lord Bridgestone, her face pale but her eyes sparkling with joy.

"My dear Marianne," Philip replied, turning towards her. "I would never have turned my back on you again, not even for a moment. You know how deeply I regretted my foolish behaviour when news of our betrothal first came to light. I am only sorry that I could not come to you before now but, as you might have heard, I was injured and had to regain some of my strength."

Miss Weston swallowed and closed her eyes for a moment, a single tear running down her cheek. The noise of the guests, the music from the orchestra, the hubbub of conversation, it all began to fade from Philip's ears. To him, there was nothing more than himself and Marianne.

"I do love you, Galsworthy."

Her quiet words spoken to him alone, sounding to Philip as though they had been shouted aloud from one side of the room to the other, his breath catching in his chest.

"You know that I –"

"May I make an announcement, ladies and gentlemen?"

Suddenly, the noise of the ballroom returned to Philip's ears with a crash, making him jerk violently. Marianne jumped also as they were both pulled from their joyous moment by the sound of Lord Henry's voice.

His heart began to beat frantically in his chest as the orchestra quietened, the voices around him dropped to a whisper, and Lord Henry climbed the stairs so that he might see as many guests as possible.

"My dear guests, how glad I am to have you all here with me this evening, on what is the most delightful of occasions," Lord Henry began with a broad smile on his face. "This is a most special night, for this is the night that I have become the happiest gentleman in all of England."

Philip dragged air into his lungs, all too aware of what the gentleman was about to do. He turned to look at Marianne and saw her staring at Lord Henry with wide eyes, the color draining from her face.

She understood what Lord Henry's plan was but, as yet, there was nothing either of them could do to prevent it.

"Miss Marianne Weston," Lord Henry continued, his voice echoing across the room. "That wonderful, beautiful creature, has agreed this very evening to be my bride."

The crowd gasped and then began to applaud as Lord Henry inclined his head as though to thank them all.

"Where are you, my dear lady?" he called, his eyes searching for her amongst the crowd. "Do come and stand next to me, my love. Let everyone see just how happy you are."

Blood roared in Philip's ears as he looked at Marianne who was now surrounded by a group of ladies, all congratulating her and grasping her hands in delight. Her eyes were not on Lord Henry but on him, glistening with tears.

"Did you know this was to occur?"

Philip turned his head to see Lord Bridgestone bearing down on him, his eyes dark with anger.

"Did you know Lord Henry had asked her, Lord Galsworthy? And did you know that she had accepted him, intending to come here this evening and disrupt her happiness in one last, desperate attempt?"

Philip shook his head, gesturing towards Marianne, who was, somehow, being taken towards Lord Henry by the well-wishers who had surrounded her. Evidently, Lord Bridgestone had not heard Marianne profess her love for Philip and given all that had occurred of late, Philip could not blame the gentleman for being entirely confused. "Look at your daughter, Lord Bridgestone. Tell me if that is delight you see on her face. Everything I have told you is true. I may not have behaved in the way you expected and certainly I did not behave in the way Marianne deserved, but I came here to prove my love for her and my determination to make her my wife." In truth, Philip was now not at all sure what he ought to do, given that his plan to reveal Lord Henry's deceit and cowardice to the *ton* had now just been torn in two by what Lord Henry himself had done.

Lord Bridgestone frowned, but nodded. "You are quite right there, Lord Galsworthy. No, she does not look at all happy." He turned his eyes back towards Philip and fixed his gaze onto him, forcing Philip to return the look despite his desire to keep his eyes on Marianne.

"You must stop this then, Lord Galsworthy. If she is

to be yours and if you love her as you state, then ensure Lord Henry has no hold on her any longer. Let the *ton* see that it is *you* who is to marry her, not Lord Henry. I do not like scandal and this, I know, will bring a good deal of gossip with it, but it is better than a broken engagement."

Awash with relief, Philip grasped Lord Bridgestone's hand for a moment. "Thank you, Lord Bridgestone," he said firmly before making to step away. "Have no doubt. I will set this all to rights."

"And set Lord Henry in his place, I have no doubt," Lord Bridgestone muttered just as Philip turned away to follow after Marianne.

CHAPTER NINETEEN

"*My* y dear lady."

Marianne swallowed hard, coming to a dead stop just at the bottom of the staircase. Lord Henry was standing only a few steps above, holding out his hand to her, but she did not want to go to him. She had not intended to come anywhere near the man, in fact, but the ladies who had come to wish her well had, in their kindness, managed to force her feet in his direction.

"Come and join me, Miss Weston," Lord Henry continued in a voice loud enough for almost all his guests to hear. The room had come to a complete standstill with every single face turned in Lord Henry's direction. Marianne fought the sudden panic that rushed through her, turning desperately to see if Lord Galsworthy had any intention of coming to her aid. After what she had just heard from him, after what she had just come to understand, the last thing she wanted was to go anywhere near Lord Henry.

"Stop, Redmond!"

Relief washed through her on hearing Lord Galsworthy's voice, seeing him striding towards her through the crowd. The guests opened up for him, their eyes alighting with wonder as they realized that something utterly sensational was about to occur right before their very eyes. Marianne was quite sure that this happiness was simply because there would be fresh gossip with which they might talk for several days, but she found she did not care one jot. All she wanted was to be freed from Lord Henry's tightening grip.

"Miss Weston."

Lord Henry's voice was hard and, to her horror, she felt a hand grip her shoulder painfully, making her twist around to face him.

"Come, my dear, away from Lord Galsworthy," Lord Henry hissed, moving his hand now to grasp her arm and half dragging her up the stairs. "We are to make our announcement and you, my dear girl, are to be filled with happiness at this wonderful news."

"No!"

She tugged her hand away from him, eliciting a gasp from the crowd only to stumble down the steps from where Lord Henry had dragged her. Lord Galsworthy was there in a moment, his hands catching her carefully and tugging her away from Lord Henry. Blinking in confusion, Marianne saw her father dart up the staircase with a good deal more vigour than she had ever expected of him, forcing himself in front of Lord Henry and preventing the gentleman from following both herself and Lord Galsworthy.

"Marianne," Lord Galsworthy said at once, turning

her away from Lord Henry. "Is this what you want?" His eyes searched her desperately. "Do you wish to be freed from me? I know that there are so many things that have occurred of late, so many things that will bring you nothing but confusion and upset, but it has been Lord Henry's doing and nothing more. I have longed to be by your side, afraid that your pain and confusion would turn you from me altogether, but I pray now that you will see the truth for what it is. I love you desperately, Marianne. I should have proposed to you long ago and I do so now."

Again, a few gasps from the guests nearby met her ears but she did not react to them at all. Her eyes were filled with nothing but Lord Galsworthy her heart finally filling with the joy and happiness she had longed for.

"I understand everything," she said, her hands finding his and holding them tightly. "I heard what you said to my father, Lord Galsworthy. I can see now that Lord Henry was determined to pull us from one another and I will not let him succeed. My heart is yours. You cannot know how much joy you bring me, Lord Galsworthy."

His smile made her heart sing.

"Then you will be my bride?" he asked hoarsely just as Lord Henry managed to release himself from Lord Bridgestone's attempts to block his way.

"Yes," she replied, wishing she might press her lips to his regardless of the crowd. "Yes, Lord Galsworthy, I will marry you."

"No!"

Marianne gasped in horror as Lord Henry's hand

grasped Lord Galsworthy's shoulder, forcing him to let out a cry of agony and twist away from her.

"No," Lord Henry breathed as the guests watched on in growing horror. "No, Miss Weston. You have already agreed to be my bride. You will not wed Lord Galsworthy."

Marianne stepped back out of his reach. "No, Lord Henry, I will not," she said in as clear a voice as she could. "You have done your utmost to break apart the betrothal between myself and Lord Galsworthy, but I declare to you here and now, that you have failed."

Lord Henry's face darkened, his lips twisting into a cruel smile. "Lord Galsworthy rejected you already, Miss Weston. He is an ill man. You deserve better."

"I am not ill," Lord Galsworthy tried to shout, now hanging onto the staircase rail with one hand pressed hard against his shoulder. His face was haggard with pain, his colour gone. Marianne made to move towards him only for Lord Henry to step into her way. Her chin lifted. She was not about to allow this gentleman, this foul-hearted, despicable creature, to get the better of her now. Looking over his shoulder at her father, she saw him nod gently, clearly giving her his blessing in her choice to wed Lord Galsworthy. Relief filled her. Looking into Lord Henry's eyes, she saw the darkness there, the malice and the deep, unrelenting arrogance that made him believe he ought to have whomever and whatever he wished. What he had done to Lord Galsworthy only proved his selfishness and cruelty, and she was not about to allow his deeds to remain unknown.

The thought hit her quickly and, moving as fast as

she could, she hurried past Lord Henry and came to stand beside her father. Lord Henry turned back towards her, but her father, as she had expected, moved to her other side, protecting her from the man. Marianne looked out at the assembled crowd, aware that they were all quite captivated by what was playing out directly in front of their eyes. Despite the fact that she found their interest so intense, she forced herself to remain steady, knowing that this was the only opportunity she would have to set things to rights in as clear and in as concise a manner as possible.

"Ladies and gentlemen," she began in as loud a voice as she dared. "Lord Galsworthy and I have been betrothed for some time, although it has not been known to anyone but our own families. Therefore, I am delighted to announce that, within the month, Lord Galsworthy and I will wed."

A smattering of applause broke from the crowd.

"However," she continued as Lord Henry attempted to move past Lord Bridgestone. "Lord Henry Redmond has attempted to ingratiate himself into our family and, deciding that *he* wished for my hand in marriage, attempted to gravely injure Lord Galsworthy so that he might be free to pursue my hand without any hindrance."

A gasp of astonishment came from the guests with many immediately turning to those around them and beginning to discuss this new, astonishing news.

"He has spoken lies to my father and to myself," Marianne finished, seeing Lord Henry's furious expression. "I must warn you all to take care of your daughters, your sisters, your nieces, when it comes to this gentleman.

Be on your guard and do not accept his acquaintance. His cruelty is quite beyond measure and yet see how stealthily he hides it."

"You are speaking untruths!" Lord Henry shouted, his hands curling into fists by his sides. "I have done no such thing, Miss Weston! How can you speak such lies?"

Marianne made to speak, only for her father to hold up a hand, silencing both her and the crowd. Every eye was on him, seeing the grave expression on the gentleman's face as he turned to Lord Henry. Even Lord Henry himself seemed to feel the gravity of the moment, for he swallowed hard and stepped back, his eyes darting from one side of the room to the other. Surely, Marianne thought to herself, surely, he must know that he is quite undone. Surely he must understand that there can be no coming back from this.

"I have heard you speak many words, Lord Henry," Lord Bridgestone began, his voice quiet and yet seeming to echo across the room. "I believed you to be a gentleman of quality and yet I discover that you have not only supposedly proposed to my daughter, but that she has accepted you – and you have not once come to my door in order to seek my permission to do so." Lord Henry immediately began to protest, but Lord Bridgestone held up his hand, silencing him. "Even if you state, Lord Henry, that my daughter accepted your proposal, I would never believe you over her words," he continued, glancing back at her. "Which makes me question just *what* I can believe."

Marianne put one hand on her father's arm, squeezing it gently. To hear her father speak up in her defense brought such joy to her heart that she thought she might burst into tears right there in front of them all.

"You told me that Lord Galsworthy was unwell," Lord Bridgestone continued, patting Marianne's hand for a moment. "You told me that he was gone to his estate, leaving my daughter behind. Now, it appears, you have lied to me about Lord Galsworthy simply to try to secure my daughter's hand."

Lord Henry was, by this point, now looking rather desperate. His eyes were darting from one place to the next, his cheeks burning with a redness that spoke of shame. "No, indeed, I still believe that Lord Galsworthy is terribly unwell. I truly did believe that he had gone to his estate and I am, as you are, most surprised to see him present with us." He shrugged, a harsh, guttural laugh escaping his mouth. "It was a simple mistake, Lord Bridgestone, that is all."

Silence fell across the entire room. Marianne's heart began to beat so loudly that she was quite sure the other guests could hear it, her stomach tightening painfully. Her father could easily accept Lord Henry's words, believing that it was a simple mistake, or he could look past the excuse and see the truth of Lord Henry's character.

"Tell me, Redmond," her father said in a stern voice. "If you did not shoot Lord Galsworthy, if you had nothing whatsoever to do with the injury to his shoulder, then tell me this: how did you know exactly where to press so that Lord Galsworthy might be weakened with the pain of it? How did you know that putting your hand on his shoulder and pressing on it, as you did, would bring so much agony to him, turning him away from my daughter?"

Lord Henry's eyes widened, his mouth falling open for a moment. He tried to say something, tried to find some excuse, but nothing came. The crowd began to mutter darkly, their consideration of his character becoming more and more apparent with every second that passed. Her father had made it quite plain to them all that Lord Henry was every bit the villain that Marianne and Lord Galsworthy had made him out to be. There was no excuse now. There was nothing for him to say in his own defense. The matter was closed. He would no longer present any sort of challenge to them.

To Marianne's surprise, Lord Henry suddenly turned on his heel and ran down the steps, back into the ballroom. Shouting angrily at people to remove themselves from his path, elbowing some as he did so, he half ran towards the open French doors and scurried out into the darkness. Marianne stared after him for a moment, not quite sure what had occurred.

"A coward," her father spat with a good degree of anger. "Nothing more than a coward. Good riddance to him." Turning, he took her hands in his, his lips in a tight line and his eyes blazing with a deep fury that Marianne knew would take some time to dissipate. "I am sorry, my dear," he finished. "I ought to have given you more consideration than I did. I thought Lord Henry to be a wonderful gentleman and now it appears..."

Trailing off, he shook his head, his frustration evident. "I should have done better for you, Marianne."

"No." She smiled and pressed one hand to his cheek

for a moment, seeing the way his anger began to fade from his eyes. "No, Father, you need not berate yourself. You have done very well for me. Lord Galsworthy has proved himself to me in a way I could never have imagined. I love him most dearly, Father. More than I can express. I know I will be happy, settled and content, and what more can one wish for than that?"

Her father drew in a long breath and patted her hand gently. "Go to him then, my dear. Go to your betrothed. I am happier for you than I can say."

Ignoring the hubbub that the dramatic events had caused, Marianne pressed her father's hand gently and then turned towards Lord Galsworthy. He had managed to rise, one hand still pressed to his shoulder. His hand was tight on the rail, the only evidence of his pain and weakness, but the love in his eyes was shining out towards her, filling her with a deep sense of happiness.

He held a hand out to her and she took it at once, a sigh of contentment leaving her lips. This was the end of what had been a terrible struggle. Their life together could soon begin, and Marianne knew that they would live a life filled with love, with affection, and with happiness. Her joy was complete.

EPILOGUE

"*My* dear lady."

Marianne jumped and let out a squeak of surprise, turning her head to see Lord Galsworthy standing in the doorway of the drawing room, holding a bunch of beautiful red roses in his hand.

"Oh, Galsworthy," she exclaimed, getting to her feet as he swept towards her. "Thank you. They are beautiful."

"Not as beautiful as you," he replied gallantly, handing them to her. She smiled up at him before pressing her nose into the blooms, their fragrance filling the room. A small sigh of happiness escaped her as she set them down on a nearby table, reminding herself to have the maids take proper care of them later.

"I have some news for you," Lord Galsworthy said reaching for her hand. "News that I hope will bring you joy."

She looked up at him, her stomach swirling with excitement. "Oh?"

"The banns have been called," he stated, reaching for her hand. "I was not present, of course, but I have been duly informed that the parish is terribly excited about it all."

Marianne smiled, her fingers twining into his. "Thank you, Galsworthy," she murmured, thinking just how wonderful a gentleman he was. They had thought, initially, to marry in London, given that both of their families were here in town already. Harriet and Lord Bridgestone would be returning to London thereafter for the little Season. Knowing just how much it would mean to her to be married from her own home, Lord Galsworthy had insisted that they all make their way to Lord Bridgestone's estate. The banns had been called there, as expected, which meant that in two short weeks, Lord Galsworthy and she would become husband and wife.

"There is nothing I would not do for you, my love," Lord Galsworthy replied, one hand now loosening from her hand and resting gently on her shoulder, his fingers brushing her neck and making her shiver. "I have given you my heart, as foolish and as ignorant as I am, and it shall never belong to another." His hand slid down her back and around her waist, drawing her a little closer to him. Marianne went willingly, her free hand now resting gently on his chest, aware of just how much his closeness affected her. A fortnight seemed almost too long to be apart from him, she realized, almost desperate to be with him without ever having to part again.

"I love you with everything I have, with everything I am, Marianne," Lord Galsworthy whispered, leaning forward. "You have forgiven me my foolishness and taken me back into your arms, back into your heart. You are everything to me, my love. I will love you every moment of our lives together."

Marianne tried to reply but found she could not. Lord Galsworthy's face was inches from her own, her breathing ragged as his lips brushed hers gently. She held her breath, closing her eyes and tilting her face up to his – only for his lips to descend again, but this time, with a good deal more firmness than before. He lingered, his arms tightening around her waist as her own hands swept around his neck. His kiss was warm and soft, sweetness and passion combining together. When he lifted his lips from hers, she let her head rest against his, knowing that this was where she belonged.

"I love you, Philip," she whispered, feeling the way his heart beat along with her own.

"And I love you, Marianne," he replied before his lips sought hers once more.

I am glad the wait is over for Philip and Marianne. Check out the next book in the series, The Long Return! Preview coming up!

MY DEAR READER

Thank you for reading and supporting my books! I hope this story brought you some escape from the real world into the always captivating Regency world. A good story, especially one with a happy ending, just brightens your day and makes you feel good! If you enjoyed the book, would you leave a review on Amazon? Reviews are always appreciated.

Below is a complete list of all my books! Why not click and see if one of them can keep you entertained for a few hours?

Saved by the Scoundrel
Mending the Duke
The Baron's Malady

The Returned Lords of Grosvenor Square
The Returned Lords of Grosvenor Square: A Regency
Romance Boxset
The Waiting Bride
The Long Return
The Duke's Saving Grace
A New Home for the Duke

The Spinsters Guild
The Spinsters Guild: A Sweet Regency Romance Boxset
A New Beginning
The Disgraced Bride
A Gentleman's Revenge
A Foolish Wager
A Lord Undone

Convenient Arrangements
Convenient Arrangements: A Regency Romance
Collection
A Broken Betrothal
In Search of Love
Wed in Disgrace
Betrayal and Lies
A Past to Forget
Engaged to a Friend

Landon House

Novellas
A Family for Christmas
Mistletoe Magic: A Regency Romance
Heart, Homes & Holidays: A Sweet Romance Anthology

Happy Reading!

All my love,

Rose

A SNEAK PEEK OF THE LONG RETURN

PROLOGUE

"Where are you?"

Little Arabella Marchmont, daughter to the Earl of Blackford, giggled as she ran as fast as she could across the garden lawn, hearing her friend shouting out after her. Practically throwing herself into the little arbour and not caring at all about the state of her dress, eight-year-old Arabella tried not to make a sound.

"I'm going to find you!"

Trying hard not to giggle, Arabella clamped one hand over her mouth. Jacob St. Leger, the second son of the Duke of Crestwick, was trying to find her in their game of 'hide and go seek', but this time she was sure he'd never be able to work out where she was.

"I'm getting closer."

Arabella let out a shriek of surprise as his voice rippled through the arbour, making Jacob laugh as he poked her in the back with his finger.

"Found you."

Arabella laughed and sat up, shaking her head as her dark ringlets danced around her face. "You always know where I am."

Jacob grinned at her, his light brown eyes glowing with happiness, a sprinkling of freckles over his nose that had been brought about by the hours they had spent playing in the sunshine.

"I'll always know where you are, Arabella," he said, sitting down next to her and grinning. "There's just something about you that always tells me where you're hiding."

Arabella rolled her eyes, her grin never fading. "I think you're peeking when you're meant to be counting."

"How dare you?" Jacob said, in mock horror. "I'd never do that." Laughing, he rose to his feet, his mop of brown hair sticking up in every direction. "Listen, I'll give you another chance, will I? I swear not to peek."

Arabella stuck out her tongue. "I knew you were cheating."

He grinned at her. "Go on then. Run. I'll count to twenty and then come after you." Leaning in closer, he winked at her. "But I'll still be able to find you."

"Not this time!" Arabella declared, her heart beating frantically as she ran away from the arbour, trying to work out where she could hide so that Jacob couldn't find her. His voice floated towards her as she hurried away, hearing him counting. Surely, she'd be able to find somewhere better to conceal herself this time?

≈

"You've never been much good at hiding."

Surprised, Arabella looked up from her book, her eyes widening at the sight of Jacob St. Leger leaning lazily against one side of the arbour.

"Jacob!"

Throwing her book aside, she practically launched himself into his arms, more delighted than she could say to see him again. "Jacob!" she exclaimed, as he held her tightly against him. "When did you get back from town?"

He grinned at her as she looked up into his face. "This morning," he said, with a laugh. "But I couldn't wait to come by. Your mother tells me that you were meant to be entertaining Lord Fairweather this morning but that you pleaded a headache and went in search of some quiet solitude in order to help it dissipate." His brow arched, making her laugh. "I know you too well to believe that, Arabella."

"You have me found out," Arabella admitted, with a wry smile. "Lord Fairweather is quite set on having me as his wife, and I'm afraid I will not accept him, even though mama thinks he is quite amiable."

Jacob grinned, tipping his head as he let her go, coming to sit down beside her. "A little too dull for you, was he?"

Arabella rolled her eyes. "Terribly so."

"And you are, therefore, avoiding him."

"Of course." She sighed happily and pressed his arm. "I am so glad to see you again, Jacob." Her eyes took him in, seeing him for the man he had become instead of the young boy she had once known. He still had those laughing brown eyes, the scattering of freckles across the bridge of his nose, but he was taller than she now, with broad shoulders and a strong back which gave him the appearance of strength and bravery. She was quite proud of him in a sisterly sort of way, even though she knew that his father disapproved of some of his son's wilder ways. How often had he come back to the garden to play or spend time with her, sad because his father had chided him once again for being less than inclined towards his lessons, and more interested in being out of doors?

"As I am you," Jacob replied, with a touch of tenderness in his voice. "Arabella, I have been thinking."

"Oh?" She twinkled up at him. "You know that can be remarkably dangerous, do you not?"

He rolled his eyes at her teasing. "Do let us try to be serious for even a short time, my dearest Arabella."

She tried not to smile, setting her hands in her lap, and fixing her eyes on his. "But of course."

To her surprise, Jacob appeared to be in deep thought for a few moments, for he leaned forward to rest his elbows on his knees and let out a long sigh. "As you know, Arabella, father wished me to go to London for the Season so that I might consider my future." His face lifted towards hers. "I have been considering it. Arabella, I want my future to be with you."

She stared at him, a little confused.

"Let me be clear," he stated, a little more firmly. "Arabella, I want you to be my bride. I want to marry you."

Blinking rapidly, Arabella narrowed her eyes as she looked into her friend's face. They had been fast friends for so many years and he was always doing something to tease her. Was this his way of doing so now?

"You are toying with me," she said, slowly, quite certain that he was trying to make her fall into some sort of trap or other, so that he could laugh at her long and hard later. "You are teasing me, are you not? My goodness, Jacob, I will not fall for such nonsense!"

Jacob frowned, his expression growing a little darker. "I am not jesting, Arabella. Can you not see that I care for you deeply?"

"Now I know for certain that you are teasing me," she said, stoutly, getting to her feet and refusing to allow him to goad her any longer. "Just because I have rejected Lord Fairweather does not mean that you must then attempt to make a joke of such things as marriage and the like. Goodness me, Jacob, I have never known you to try and make light of such serious things as matrimony before." She tossed her head, her ringlets no longer bouncing around her face but rather held back neatly. "I consider your jokes in rather poor taste." Walking out to the gardens, she looked over her shoulder, expecting Jacob to come running after her, a broad grin on his face as he confessed that he had been doing just that.

To her surprise, he did not follow her.

Shrugging, Arabella hastened back to the house, telling herself that Jacob was being much too ridiculous to try to make her believe that such an offer was genuine. He was always playing tricks on her and trying to make her believe whatever it was he wished her to believe, but he would not be successful here. She knew him too well for that and if he wished to sulk over the fact that he had failed terribly, then she was not about to feel any sort of sympathy for him.

Arabella did not give the arbour a single glance over her shoulder, despite her frustrated thoughts towards him. If she had, she might have seen Jacob St. Leger standing by it, his expression utterly wretched, as he watched her walk away.

CHAPTER ONE

Eight months later

"Have any letters arrived today?"

The maid shook her head as she finished dressing Arabella's hair.

"No, my lady."

Arabella's heart sank low, just as it had done every day since she had last seen Jacob in the arbour.

"I will inform you the moment anything arrives," the maid said, encouragingly, as she stepped back. "There, my lady. I think you are ready."

Arabella nodded, not even looking at her reflection in the mirror. "I thank you."

The maid bobbed a curtsy. "Is there anything else?"

"No," Arabella replied, dully. "There is not." She waited until the maid had quit the room before rising to her feet and making her way to her music box, where she kept her most precious possessions.

Carefully lifting the lid, she took out the same small letter that she had read every day since Jacob had left, sitting down on her bed to unfold it.

Her eyes dragged over the words written there, even though she already knew them by heart.

"I am to leave England," she read aloud. "The second son of a Duke must have some occupation and so I have had my father purchase colours for me. I do not know when I will return." Her breath caught, grief tearing at her heart as she read the final two sentences. "I have loved you for a long time, Arabella, and my proposal was truly what I desired. How broken I am to realise that such a thing can never be."

Her voice cracked, tears pricking at her eyes as she lowered her head, her grief growing all the more as she thought of her dear friend. Jacob, who had meant so much to her, and whose proposal she had thought of as nothing more than a jest on his part, had turned away from her entirely. He had joined the army and she did not know where he had gone.

Of course, she had written to him almost immediately, but had received a note from the Duke of Crestwick, Jacob's father, to inform her that Jacob was already gone, but that he would forward the letter to London. She could not be sure whether or not Jacob had ever received her letter and yet, even though it had been eight months since their parting, she waited in hope every day for a reply.

Oh, how she had begged him to return to her! How

she had wept as she had looked into the depths of her heart and realised that none but Jacob would do for her. To know that his proposal had been genuine, that his words had been true, had quite broken her heart into pieces, regret and disappointment filling every part of her being.

Letting out a long breath and battling against the tears that threatened, Arabella settled her shoulders and fixed her gaze on the window. The dull spring sunshine was doing its best to cheer her, but it was not enough to bring a smile to her face. Instead, she felt her soul grow weary, a heavy weight bearing down upon it.

Knowing that her mother would be expecting her presence at the breakfast table, Arabella rose to her feet and set the letter back in the music box, letting her fingers trace it for just another moment before she closed the lid. She would read his letter again tomorrow, sending up a silent prayer for his safe return *and* for his forgiveness when the time came. She had to hope that she was not too late to accept his proposal, had to believe that their friendship would be enough to sustain them.

Making her way below stairs, Arabella heard her mother speak sharply to her older sister, Martha, wincing at the harsh tone. Martha, however, did not appear to be too perturbed, for she replied calmly, evidently refuting whatever it was her mother had said. Arabella wished she too could speak to her mother with such surety but she found the sting of her mother's hard words often too difficult to bear. Her mother, Lady Blackford, had become all the more difficult since her husband and Arabella's father, had died some seven months ago. Arabella had tried her best to be understanding and sympathetic, especially in light of her mother's grief, but as time had gone on, her mother appeared to be getting worse instead of improving.

"Ah, Arabella, there you are," her mother said, her thin face as pale as ever, although her dark eyes were narrowed with frustration and anger. "Come, we must go in. Rosalind will be waiting."

Rosalind *was* waiting, even though she did not appear to mind. Instead, she sent a warm glance in Martha's direction, as though to encourage her. Arabella ignored this, knowing that out of the three of them, she was the only one who was not attached in some way.

Both Rosalind and Martha were betrothed, although the weddings would not take place until after their year of mourning was ended. Their father, Lord Blackford, had not only approved of the marriages but had been quite resounding in his encouragement of them, for he had declared himself to be a great believer that love between husband and wife was the only thing of importance.

Martha was to marry a second son without title or particular wealth, who hailed from Covent Garden. Rosalind was to marry Baron Southend, which, to her mother's mind at least, was better than no title at all! Whilst Arabella was glad for her sisters, their happiness only made her own discontent and regret all the more obvious.

"Do not eat too much this morning, Arabella," her mother instructed, as Arabella rose to fill her plate from the dishes that had been laid out on the sideboard. "I must say, we will soon have to send for the seamstress to let your dresses out if you continue on as you are!"

Arabella closed her eyes tightly, battling her anger. Her mother always had something to say about her behaviour, her dress, or her manner, and she was growing rather tired of it.

"Mama, you need not chide Arabella so," Martha interjected, softly, although there was a strength in her voice. "She is not a child."

Lady Blackford snorted. "She has made foolish decisions, just as a child might do."

Deeply regretting that she had ever informed her mother about what Jacob had said, Arabella whirled around to face her mother, the empty plate being gently taken from her hands by Rosalind. "Mama, that is more than enough," Arabella said, heat crawling up into her cheeks as she battled with her anger. "Do you not think that I am tortured enough already? Do you not consider how I must live with my regret every single day?"

Her mother sniffed and looked away, as though she found Arabella's display of emotion a little improper.

"I am waiting for Jacob to return from war so that we might make amends," Arabella continued, aware that her voice was rising but finding that she did not care. "I am saddened over his parting, I am grief-stricken over the loss of our dear father." Something flickered in her mother's eyes as she looked back sharply at Arabella, her face going suddenly pale.

"Therefore," Arabella finished, feeling a small sense of triumph. "I shall eat what I please, dress how I please and act as I please. I have had more than enough chiding from you, mama. Leave me to myself, I beg you, for I cannot bear any more of your sharp tongue."

So saying, she turned around and practically snatched the plate from her sister's hand, filling it up with more food than she would ever manage to finish eating. She just wanted to show her mother that her words meant nothing to Arabella.

For the next half hour, breakfast went without argument, without harsh words being spoken and without the appearance of malice. Arabella was mostly silent, as was her mother, although when Martha and Rosalind began to discuss their upcoming weddings, Arabella felt as though she could bear no more and rose from her chair.

"I think I will take my tea in the drawing room," she said, by way of explanation. "If you will excuse me."

She hurried towards the door, praying that she would not be followed, only for her mother to call her name as she came out after her.

Arabella closed her eyes. "Yes, mama?"

Lady Blackford did not look to be angry, although her expression was rather tense.

"Arabella, you must consider your future."

Wishing she could groan aloud, Arabella did not stop in her attempts to reach the drawing-room unhindered. She walked quickly, ignoring her mother as she hurried alongside her.

"You must marry!"

Arabella let out a sharp breath, swung around on her heel and planted her hands on her hips. "Why must I? As I have said before, I am waiting for Jacob's return."

"You cannot wait that long," her mother said, decisively. "I am aware that the Duke of Crestwick has recently lost his eldest son and that they hope for St. Leger's return so that he might take up his duties as the new heir, but that is beside the point. Your sisters are both to wed very soon – although their matches are not at all what I would have chosen and they will certainly feel the folly of their choices once they are wed – therefore, it is entirely down to you to make sure this family has *some* manner of respectability."

Arabella resisted the urge to roll her eyes. "Mama, both of my sisters' beaus are quite respectable."

"That is not what I mean," Lady Blackford stated, sharply. "You are to marry a gentleman with title and wealth. You cannot wait in the hope that St. Leger will return home and, even if he did, he may no longer be interested in you, after your rejection of him."

Forcing her anger to remain under her control, Arabella chose her words carefully, growing more and more frustrated with every moment. "Mama, we are quite a respectable family. My brother will soon return from the continent to take the title and control of the estate. He will marry and produce the required heir, I am quite sure. Therefore, it does not matter who I choose to marry, just as it is not of any particular consequence who my sisters choose to wed."

"It will matter to you!" her mother exclaimed, clearly growing a little exasperated. "It will matter when you find yourself in a much poorer situation than you are at this present time, when you do not have the ease of living that you currently enjoy!" Her voice rose, her cheeks flaring with colour. "Your sisters will have that to deal

with and I know full well that they will not find it particularly easy. Love may be what guides them at this present
moment but it may not last and then what shall they do?"

Arabella pressed her lips together, lifted her chin and
looked directly into her mother's eyes. "Mama, my sisters
have made their choice. I shall make my own choice also."

Her mother blew out a breath of frustration. "You are
determined to wait, then, to see if St. Leger will give you
another chance?"

"What else can I do but that?" Arabella persisted,
wishing that her mother could understand. "First you
chide me for refusing him, which I know full well was
both foolish and misguided, and now you urge me to
forget him and seek another!" Despite herself, her eyes
filled with tears. "Why must you be so harsh with me?"

Her mother drew herself up, her expression as hard
as her words. "It is for your own good, Arabella. There is
no use in waiting for a gentleman who, I believe, will not
wish to see you again. Therefore, you must think of your
future and of this family's reputation. It is your duty."

Arabella wanted to say more but found that her heart
was beating with such torment, with such pain, that it
was all she could do to keep her composure. Making to
turn on her heel in order to leave her mother's side and
seek the quietness she required, Arabella was stopped by
the sound of running feet.

It was one of the maids.

"A letter for you, Lady Arabella."

Arabella grasped it at once, her heart beating
painfully as she looked down at the seal and saw that it
was from the Crestwick estate. She was somewhere

between hope and fear, breaking open the seal with shaking fingers and unfolding the letter carefully.

Her eyes ran over the words but her mind refused to accept them. From far away, it seemed, she heard her mother calling her name, her fingers grasping at Arabella's arm.

The world seemed to shift underneath her, her eyes losing focus as the letter slipped from her fingers. She could not believe it, could not accept it. Surely the letter could not be true, surely it could not mean that Jacob would never return. There had to be some sort of mistake. He could not be dead. He could not be gone from this place for good. It could not be.

Swaying slightly, Arabella closed her eyes and felt tears on her cheeks. Her mother put a steadying arm about Arabella's waist, urging her forward into the drawing room, until Arabella found herself resting on the *chaise longue,* her mind and heart heavy with grief, regret, and pain.

He was gone. He would not be coming back home again, would never again take her hands and smile into her eyes.

She had lost him forever.

CHAPTER TWO

Six months later

*A*rabella smiled delightedly as Martha walked back down the aisle, arm in arm with her new husband. They were looking at each other as they walked, their eyes aglow with the love they had for one another.

Mr. Brackham was not, of course, a particularly wealthy gentleman and certainly did not have any title to speak of, given that he was the second son of a viscount, but that did not seem to matter to Martha. Even though her mother had persisted with her dire warnings about Martha's difficult future, should she continue with her planned engagement to the gentleman, Martha had simply ignored her mother's words and had begun to look forward to the day she would be wed. It was a small affair but Arabella felt herself truly happy for her sister, slowly beginning to believe that Martha would have a wonderful, joyous life, even if she were not as rich as she might have been, had she married another.

Her other sister, Rosalind, sighed with contentment, putting one hand on Arabella's arm. "She looked very happy, did she not?"

"She did," Arabella agreed, looking at Rosalind and seeing the happiness and the longing in her own expression. "Your wedding is not so far off now, Rosalind. I can tell that you are as eager as Martha to wed!"

Rosalind laughed gently, her cheeks colouring. "One cannot help but be eager for one's wedding day," she replied, as the family began to file out of the church, ready to greet and congratulate Martha. "Especially if it is to be a happy affair."

"Indeed," Arabella murmured, wondering how her mother expected her to smile and laugh and engage in conversation with any of the gentlemen here when her heart was still full of Jacob. She had no interest in any of them, not when she was still lost in her grief over Jacob's death, and yet her mother had insisted that she do her utmost to acquaint herself with as many gentlemen as possible.

"You still miss him?"

"Of course I do," Arabella whispered, as Rosalind fell into step beside her. "It is quite unbearable at times, especially when mama insists that I am to wed another within the year."

Rosalind made a small sound of understanding. "Our mother has her own ideas about our happiness," she said, slowly. "Even though our brother has returned and has promised to ensure that we are all well taken care of, either through our dowry or our continued residence at the estate, mama cannot help but fear for each of us. She is doing all she can to guide us in her own way, even though she continually tries to insist that I must find a gentleman of a higher title than my Baron!"

Arabella laughed, seeing Rosalind shake her head. She knew that her sister would not be swayed, in much the same way that Martha had ignored her mother's pleas to end the engagement.

"She has nothing else to do but worry about us," Rosalind finished, as they walked outside into the sunshine. "Allow her to tell you whatever it is she wishes, but let your own heart guide you, Arabella."

"I will," Arabella promised, as they hurried towards Martha to press their congratulations on her. Her sister looked more beautiful than Arabella had ever seen her before and, even though she was grieved still over the loss of Jacob and over the reminder of what *could* have been, she did all she could to focus solely on Martha's happiness.

～

"And you are Lady Arabella, of course."

Arabella stifled a sigh as yet another gentleman came to bow over her hand, aware that her mother, who had brought each and every one over to her, was expecting her to be both charming and elegant.

"It is very good to make your acquaintance, Lord

Hartson," she said, without meaning a word of it. "How are you acquainted with the happy couple?"

Thankfully, this seemed to distract Lord Hartson from his intention to bow and scrape over Arabella's hand, for he launched into an explanation about how he knew the family of Martha's husband, going into great detail about their connection, whilst Arabella did her best to remain interested whilst inwardly dying of boredom.

Lord Hartson was, in the end, removed from her side by the sight of another young lady with whom he was acquainted. Arabella let out a sigh of relief as she smiled, thinking that none of the last five gentlemen her mother had insisted on introducing her to had been anything like Jacob St. Leger. None of them had made her smile, not one had appeared to have anything of particular interest to say and certainly she did not find even one of them to have a handsomeness about them that caught her eye.

No, none would compare to Jacob.

"Arabella, you must stop attempting to find fault with each and every gentleman I bring to you," her mother hissed, her eyes a little narrowed. "I can see what is going on inside that head of yours and it is quite ridiculous! You must forget St. Leger and allow yourself to consider your future without hinderance!"

"Then let me make my own choice when it comes to whom I speak to and whom I seek to be introduced to, mama," Arabella begged, putting a gentle hand on her mother's arm so that Lady Blackford would not think her rude. "I cannot allow my heart to free itself so soon from the love and regret that ties it."

Her mother shook her head in despair. "It is foolish to

cling onto such affections, my dear," she said, with a good deal of sympathy that surprised Arabella completely. "I know that you loved St. Leger, and that you have found it difficult to deal with the regret and the sorrow that has come with the news of his death. But you *must* not allow that to continue to hold you back. You have been six months without him, and I have allowed you that time to deal with your grief without pressing any other gentleman into your acquaintance, have I not?"

Arabella nodded, having to admit that this was the case. "Yes, mama. You have."

"Then allow me to try to guide you towards a new path," her mother continued, with more gentleness than Arabella had expected. "One that might help you to see that you can find happiness with another, even though, at the present time, you might not even wish to consider it."

Arabella closed her eyes briefly, wishing that she had simply been able to enjoy her sister's wedding breakfast without being pushed into considering her own future. "Very well, mama," she said, heavily, knowing that her mother would not accept a simple refusal. Besides which, she had to admit that Lady Blackford *had* left her quite alone for the last few months, not at all insisting that Arabella forget Jacob St. Leger immediately or trying to further introductions with any particular gentlemen. Perhaps her mother was right, as much as Arabella did not want to admit it. "Although I pray that you will only introduce me to one or two more, mama. I am growing a little weary of new introductions!"

Her mother hid a smile, although there was a gleam of triumph in her sharp eyes. "Very good," she stated, quietly. "Now, come with me. The Earl of Winchester has been eager to make your acquaintance but he has been quite caught up in conversation with Lady Petronella, but I see now that he is gone from her side. *Do* hurry up, Arabella, and try to smile. The Earl of Winchester is both handsome and wealthy and may very well do for you!"

But he will never be Jacob.

Thrusting that thought aside, Arabella walked alongside her mother towards the Earl of Winchester, allowing herself to study the gentleman as she did so. He had the bearing of a wealthy and titled gentleman, and there was a kindness in his smile that appeared to reach his bright blue eyes. He was rather stocky and not overly tall, which was quite the opposite of Jacob. Thick, fair hair was swept back from his forehead, giving the Earl an almost regal appearance.

She felt a small swirl of nervousness as her mother greeted the Earl warmly, wondering why such a gentleman had been eager to make her acquaintance.

"My lord, allow me to introduce my youngest daughter, Lady Arabella."

The Earl's eyes flickered with interest as Arabella curtsied, leaving him a little tardy when it came to his own bow.

"How very good to make your acquaintance at last, Lady Arabella," he said, his voice warm. "I was introduced to your sister some years ago, and your mother also. Although I do not think you were in London at that time."

Arabella smiled tightly, seeing her mother's sharp

look. "Indeed," she murmured, knowing that she had never sought to be introduced to any particular gentleman, regardless of his title or wealth. "I may have not yet been out, my lord."

The Earl looked a little abashed, but then set his shoulders. "Well, I am very glad to make your acquaintance now, Lady Arabella. The rumours about your beauty are, I am glad to say, all quite true."

Arabella looked up at him in surprise, a little taken aback at such a compliment. "I thank you," she murmured, aware that her mother was slowly backing away so that she might be caught by another acquaintance and leave Arabella and the Earl alone. "You are very kind."

"But I speak the truth!" the Earl protested, as though she had refused to accept his words. "You will find, Lady Arabella, that I am not a gentleman inclined towards lying, no matter what the cause."

She lifted an eyebrow. "I did not say such a thing, my lord."

"And yet there is something in your eyes that says you are not quite as eager to accept my compliment as I had hoped," he stated as if he had been able to look into her soul and see her continued disinclination towards both his company and his conversation. "Perhaps you are unused to such praise, although I can hardly believe it."

Arabella felt a slow blush creep into her cheeks despite herself. "That may be," she replied, a little coyly. "I cannot say for certain myself."

The Earl of Winchester's smile grew. "Then I think you shall have to steel yourself against all the wonderful words of praise and even adoration that will come your way when you go to London," he stated, with a broad smile. "For you are certain to have such lavish compliments pressed upon you from every side."

Arabella blinked, a little surprised. "London?" she repeated, looking at him in confusion.

"Yes," he replied, with a chuckle. "You need not pretend, Lady Arabella, for your mother has quite given you away. I hear that you are to go to London for the Season."

"Oh." This was news to Arabella, who had not heard her mother speak of any such notion over the last few months, although she could not exactly say such a thing to Lord Winchester now. "But of course."

"Your sister is to be wed from there, I believe," Lord Winchester continued, clearly unaware of Arabella's surprise. "And then you will stay for the rest of the Season. I cannot tell you what delight this brings me."

Arabella blinked rapidly, trying to work out what her mother had said to the Earl of Winchester whilst doing her best to remain composed and entirely at her ease. To go to London for Rosalind's wedding was one thing, but to remain there for the Season was quite another. Her mother was evidently eager to have Arabella wed and settled by the year's end. Perhaps then Lady Blackford would find the peace she was so evidently without at this present moment.

"Do you think, Lady Arabella, that I might call upon you when you return to London?"

The Earl's voice was faint and Arabella had to cling on to it in order to drag herself back to the present situation instead of losing herself in confusion and doubt. "I beg your pardon? I could not quite hear you over the... din." Her cheeks burned with embarrassment. There were not a great number of guests and there certainly was not a large amount of noise from their conversation but thankfully, the Earl did not appear to notice.

"I was hoping, Lady Arabella," he said again, with his eyes fixed on her own, "that I might call upon you when you are in London. I should like to further our acquaintance."

Arabella stared up at him, her mind filling with memories. It was not the Earl that stood before her for a moment, but Jacob, his eyes bright with hope, his smile warm and loving.

And then he faded away, leaving her with the Earl of Winchester instead. He was not Jacob. He could never be Jacob and it was this knowledge that brought both a heaviness and a relief to her heart.

Yes, Jacob could never be replaced, but her mother was correct in trying to encourage her to think of what her future could be instead. The Earl appeared to be kind and well-mannered and was obviously eager to see her again - she could not simply refuse him because the man was not Jacob St. Leger. That would be quite ridiculous.

You are only going to become a little better acquainted with him, she told herself, putting a small smile on her face. *This is not a marriage proposal. It is simply a desire to get to know you a little better.*

"But of course," she found herself saying, despite her heart screaming at her that this was some sort of betrayal of Jacob. "I would like that very much, Lord Winchester."

The Earl beamed as though she had granted him some wonderful boon. "Capital, Lady Arabella," he declared, grasping her hand, and bowing over it. "I look forward to seeing you again very soon."

"Very soon," Arabella repeated, knowing that she felt none of the happiness nor the hope that Lord Winchester felt. Her heart was heavy, her hopes still dashed. Lord Winchester might be a respectable gentleman, but he would never take the place of Jacob within her heart. Jacob would always reside there, holding her grief, her regret, and her love with him. No-one else would ever compare, not even if she were married for fifty years or more. She would never be able to forget him, would never be able to allow her heart the freedom to love another.

Not even if it were the kind, handsome and rich Earl of Winchester.

What happens next with Arabella? Can she move on from Jacob? Click here to read the rest of the story!

JOIN MY MAILING LIST!

Sign up for my newsletter to stay up to date on new releases, contests, giveaways, freebies, and deals!

Free book with signup!

Monthly Facebook Giveaways! Books and Amazon gift cards!
Join me on Facebook: https://www.
facebook.com/rosepearsonauthor

Website: www.RosePearsonAuthor.com

Follow me on Goodreads: Author Page

You can also follow me on Bookbub!
Click on the picture below – see the Follow button?

JOIN MY MAILING LIST!

Made in the USA
Las Vegas, NV
12 March 2023

68976750R00142